"Remember our first kiss? I do."

Looking into his sexy hazel eyes with sinfully long lashes, she drew a deep breath because it felt as if all the air in the diner had suddenly vanished. She couldn't keep from glancing at Tom's mouth, thinking about his kisses, remembering them in exacting detail and wanting to kiss him now.

"Of course I do, but I'm surprised you do."

"I do. Why do you think I asked you out again?" he said, those hazel eyes twinkling, and she felt a tug on her heartstrings because she remembered again what fun she'd had with him.

"It was all exciting, Tom," she said with regret.

"Then don't cry about it now. Happy memories. Take the ones that were special and exciting and concentrate on them."

"Thank you," she said, smiling at him as he released her.

Right away, she missed his strong arms around her.

* * *

Reunited with the Rancher is part of the series Texas Cattleman's Club: Blackmail—

No secret—or heart—is safe in Royal, Texas...

Dear Reader,

In this story, meet Emily and Tom Knox, two more members of the Texas Cattleman's Club from Royal, Texas. Deeply in love, Emily and Tom were torn apart by the accidental death of their first child— little four-year-old Ryan—an incredibly devastating loss that never stops hurting. Tom and Emily share a Texas ranch and Tom moved to the guesthouse, leaving Emily alone in their palatial ranch home.

At the opening of the story, they have been estranged over a year when Emily is stunned to open a letter with a hateful message from a troll. The message with an attached picture is another knife to her heart from a blackmailer who has been hurting members of the Texas Cattleman's Club. Because of the secrets in that message, Tom comes back into Emily's life and gradually they each discover their love may still be alive.

They have to work through their loss, their love, the mistakes they've made in dealing with this tragedy and with each other. They realize the attraction they felt has grown, yet neither one knows whether their love is sufficient enough to forge a new life together.

Thank you for your interest in this book and best wishes to you,

Sara Orwig

SARA ORWIG

———

REUNITED WITH THE RANCHER

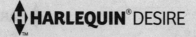

HARLEQUIN® DESIRE

Special thanks and acknowledgment are given to Sara Orwig for her contribution to the Texas Cattleman's Club: Blackmail miniseries.

Recycling programs for this product may not exist in your area.

ISBN-13: 978-0-373-83831-8

Reunited with the Rancher

Copyright © 2017 by Harlequin Books S.A.

This edition published by arrangement with Harlequin Books S.A.

For questions and comments about the quality of this book, please contact us at CustomerService@Harlequin.com.

www.Harlequin.com

Printed in U.S.A.

Sara Orwig is an Oklahoman whose life revolves around family, flowers, dogs and books. Books are like her children: she usually knows where they are, they delight her and she doesn't want to be without them. With a master's degree in English, Sara has written mainstream fiction, and historical and contemporary romance. She has one hundred published novels translated in over twenty-six languages. You can visit her website at saraorwig.com.

Books by Sara Orwig

Harlequin Desire

Lone Star Legends

The Texan's Forbidden Fiancée
A Texan in Her Bed
At the Rancher's Request
Kissed by a Rancher
The Rancher's Secret Son
That Night with the Rich Rancher

Callahan's Clan

Expecting the Rancher's Child
The Rancher's Baby Bargain

Texas Cattleman's Club: Blackmail

Reunited with the Rancher

Visit her Author Profile page at Harlequin.com, or saraorwig.com, for more titles.

With many thanks to Stacy Boyd and
Charles Griemsman for working with me on this.
Thank you to Tahra Seplowin.
Also, thank you to Maureen Walters.

With love to my family—you are so special to me.

One

Tom Knox hurried down the hall of the Texas Cattleman's Club, his footsteps muffled by the thick carpet. The dark wood-paneled walls held oil paintings and two tall mirrors in wide ornate frames. There were potted palms and chairs covered in antique satin. Tom was so accustomed to his surroundings he paid no attention until a woman rounded the corner at the end of the long hall.

Tom's insides clutched and heat filled him as he looked at his estranged wife, Emily Archer Knox. Physical attraction, definitely lust, hit him as his gaze swept over her.

Wavy honey-brown hair framed her face. Her

hair was always soft to touch. There was no way to shut off the memories, no matter how much they hurt or stirred him. A red linen suit with a matching linen blouse and red high heels added to her attractiveness. The red skirt ended above her knees, leaving her shapely legs bare to her ankles. His imagination filled in how she would look without the red linen. While desire ran rampant, at the same time, a shroud of guilt enveloped him. He had failed her in the worst way possible.

Each time he saw Emily, guilt gnawed at him for failing to save the life of their four-year-old son, Ryan, after a tour bus accident on a family ski vacation in Colorado. It had been five long, guilt-ridden years since then, and a chilly bitterness had settled in between them. His life had improved only slightly last year when he'd moved out of the house to the guesthouse on their ranch. They could go for weeks without crossing paths.

In many ways it was better to be apart, because then he could let go of the burden of guilt. That's why he had joined the Army Rangers for three years after the accident. After the death of his close friend, Jeremy, he wanted out of the Rangers. He couldn't be with Emily without thinking about how he had failed her and how unhappy she had been with him.

At the moment when they approached each other, Emily looked up and her green eyes widened. They avoided each other most of the time but couldn't today. He kept walking, his heart drumming while desire and guilt continued to war within him. Would he ever be able to face her without an internal emotional upheaval? Her smile was polite, the kind of smile usually reserved for strangers. When she came closer, her smile vanished before she greeted him with a quiet, "Hi, Tom."

"Good morning. You look great," he couldn't keep from saying.

Her gaze shifted to the briefcase in his hand. "Are you at the club for a meeting?"

"Yes. The finance committee. How about you?"

"I'm having lunch with a friend," she answered. How polite they were, yet a storm was going on within him. Guilt, hurt, too much loss plagued him each time he saw Emily or talked to her.

"Have a good time," he said as he passed her.

Her perfume stirred memories of holding her in his arms while he kissed her. Longing tore at him along with anger at himself. Why couldn't he let go completely? He and Emily didn't have anything together any longer. Only he knew that wasn't true. There was one thing they still had that hadn't vanished—a physical attraction that he felt each time she came into his sight. It was something he couldn't understand and didn't want to think about.

On a physical level, he knew she felt that chem-

istry as much as he did. She couldn't hide her re-
actions completely, and neither could he. But each
time he encountered her, he was reminded that they
both needed a chance for a fresh start, and that
maybe the best thing he could do would be to give
her a divorce and get out of her life completely.

After lunch at the Texas Cattleman's Club and
an afternoon at her photography studio in down-
town Royal, Emily drove home to Knox Acres, the
cattle ranch she shared with Tom. She still couldn't
stop replaying their brief encounter at the Texas
Cattleman's Club. Since she first met him, she'd
had a strong physical reaction to Tom. She still got
tingles from just seeing him. Through good times,
through the worst of times, Tom had dazzled her
since they had fallen in love at sixteen. She had
no comparison, but she didn't think that mattered.
Tom was the best-looking, most appealing guy she
had ever known.

Even so, other aspects of their marriage out-
weighed sheer lust. And they had lost what was
essential in a marriage—that union of hearts, that
joy in each other.

Their happiness had shattered the night their
tour bus had skidded on an icy Colorado high-
way, going into a frozen pond. Tom had almost
died pulling Ryan from the frigid water. Tom had
ended up with pneumonia, a deep cut on his knee

and a broken collarbone, broken ribs and a ruptured spleen. But in the end, he hadn't been able to save their son's life. After three days Tom could travel and they flew Tom, Emily and Ryan to a big hospital in Denver. They couldn't help Ryan, either. In eight more days, Ryan succumbed to his injuries. Somehow, amid all the grief, she and Tom composed themselves long enough to donate Ryan's organs to spare other parents the agony of losing a child.

The vacation had been Tom's family reunion, and twenty-three members of his family were on the bus. Besides Ryan, Tom's aunt died from drowning. Three other people, including two children, died in the accident, but they weren't in the Knox party.

Weeks turned into months and months into years, and her memories became more precious. In an effort to strengthen their marriage, they had tried to conceive again, but a new baby—a new start—never happened for them. Emily felt she had failed Tom in this; it was another blow to their marriage. They'd lost their son, and eventually their love, and their relationship became more strained until Tom moved out and they hardly saw each other any longer. It was general knowledge with most people they knew that they were estranged. Sometimes that still shocked her as much as everything else that had happened to them. She had been so in love with Tom when they married, she never would have believed the day would come when they barely spoke and hardly saw each other.

Hoping to put Tom out of her thoughts, she talked to her big white cat that had been a kitten given to Ryan when he was four. After feeding Snowball, she turned on her computer to read her email, and in seconds, a message caught her attention.

It was harsh, simple: Guess you weren't woman enough to hold his interest. Here's his real family, his secret family—until now. Frowning and puzzled, Emily scanned the subject: Today—for your eyes only. Tomorrow—for all of Royal to see.

She froze when she read the sender's name: Maverick. She had no idea who Maverick was. No one in Royal knew the identity of the hateful troll who'd been threatening and blackmailing people in town for the past few months. There were rumors Maverick might be the work of the three snooty stepsisters—that's how she pictured the clique of women, Cecelia Morgan, Simone Parker and Naomi Price, who seemed to think they owned the Texas Cattleman's Club and everything else in Royal these days. They always made Emily feel that she wasn't good enough to be included in their company.

Another chill slithered down Emily's spine when she opened the email attachment. It was a photograph. She stared at Tom in the picture, and shock hit her. As a professional photographer, Emily knew at a glance this picture was real. A smiling, earthy redhead with her hair fastened up in a ponytail posed with Tom, who stood close and had his arm draped around her shoulders. In front of them were two adorable children. The boy she guessed to be around four—the same age their Ryan had been when they had lost him. The little red-haired girl was pretty. In the background was a gingerbread dream house and beside the boy was a show-worthy golden retriever. They looked like the perfect family.

So this was Tom's preferred family. That made her the world's biggest fool. She and her husband had been growing apart for the past five years, and now she could see an additional reason why. Fury made her hot. There was a whole different side to Tom she had never seen—a deceitful side. She had trusted him completely. She stared at the picture, which was absolute evidence that their marriage was built on lies. Tom had another family. He was leading a double life. The realization was almost a physical blow.

If she wanted proof that their marriage was irrevocably broken, she had it now. Fresh out of excuses to delay the inevitable, heartsick and furious with Tom for his deception, she could see no other option: she planned to file for divorce. She would give him his official freedom to stop being secretive about the family he loved.

Shaking with anger, she leaned in closer to the computer screen to study the photo intently. The woman looked familiar, but Emily didn't know who she was. Were she and her kids in Royal?

And was the message on target—was Emily not woman enough to hold Tom? She shivered as she admitted to herself that the message was accurate, dead-on accurate. She couldn't give Tom the family he wanted.

It had been Tom's idea to move out to the guesthouse. He'd said separating would give them a chance to think clearly about their futures. He was the one who'd said they needed to get the physical attraction out of the way so they could straighten out their emotions and feelings for each other.

Knowing the real reason Tom wanted to move out of the house, away from her, hurt Emily badly.

She looked again at the sender's email signature. She had no idea who Maverick was. Could the rumors be right, that Cecelia Morgan, Simone Parker and Naomi Price were behind the nasty emails and the blackmail? Those three were successful businesswomen, so it didn't seem likely in a lot of ways. They might be snooty, but that didn't mean they were this evil.

Someone intended to make Tom's secret public to people in Royal. When that happened, Emily

knew she would be viewed with pity and there
would be laughter behind her back. That was in-
significant next to the pain that consumed her over
Tom's deception. How could he have been so du-
plicitous? It seemed totally unlike the man she
knew and loved.

Would Maverick write Tom and threaten to go
public? Had he—or she—already tried to extort
money from Tom for silence? Emily could easily
imagine Tom telling Maverick to go to hell first.

Emily couldn't stop her tears as her growing
fury overwhelmed her. All this time, Tom had had
a wife to love, to love him in return, precious children and a home. No wonder she couldn't get back
together with him.

She intended to confront Tom with the truth.
Their marriage was over. Completely finished. She
needed a divorce to go on with her life. She had
lost their son, and evidently, she'd lost Tom long
ago, too. He was a lying, two-faced man she hadn't
ever really known. She had never suspected that
side of Tom. She had never even had a hint of it before now. Tom had seemed totally honest, kind—
how he had fooled her! She wanted to scream at
him and tell him how deceitful and hurtful he was.
She wanted him out of her life, and this would en-
sure that happened.

She spent a sleepless night and drove into Royal
the next day. Angry and hurt, she filed for divorce.

Tom was now home from the military after his tour of duty with the Rangers, and he had taken over running the ranch. She had her photography studio and had just inherited her uncle Woody's old home in Royal. She and Tom could go their separate ways.

After work later that day, she went by the three-story house she had inherited from her uncle, the man who had raised her. The house was all she had left of family, so she intended to hang on to it and restore it so she could live there. She would be close to her photography studio and off the ranch, away from Tom. She didn't want to live in the palatial house on the ranch that they had built before Ryan was born anymore.

Tom drove back to the guesthouse after working outside all day on first one job and then another. Hard physical labor was the best way to drive the hurtful memories away, at least temporarily. It was early March, and the days were growing longer and warmer. It was spring—a time that used to be exciting and filled with promise. Now one day was like another and he spent time thinking over how he should plan his future.

At the present moment he wanted a shower and a beer and wished he had someone, a friend, to spend the evening with. Nights were long and lonely, and weekends were the worst.

As he pulled up, he saw a car parked in front of his house. It surprised him even more when he realized it was Emily's.

Why was she here? She never came to see him. Worried something might have happened to a friend, he frowned. Emily really had no family—only older cousins she didn't see. He parked and stepped out, slamming the pickup door behind him. He watched her open her car door to get out. She wore stiletto heels with black straps on her shapely feet. Her jeans fit her tiny waist snugly and were tight enough to emphasize her long, long legs. She wore a pale blue short-sleeved sweater that hugged her lush curves. In jeans, high heels and the sweater, she looked stunning. Her hair fell loosely around her face—the way he liked it best.

When his gaze raked over her, his pulse jumped. In spite of all their troubles, he was as physically drawn to her as ever. She was a good-looking woman—he'd always thought so and he still did. At the sight of her, memories tormented him, moments when he'd held and kissed her and wanted her with all his being. They'd had steamy nights of sexy loving, exciting days filled with happiness—a time that seemed incredibly far away and impossible to find ever again. He had failed her in the biggest possible way and now their love had ended. They had been through too much upheaval and loss to ever regain what they'd had.

Even so, desire for Emily was intense. He remembered that silky curtain of honey-brown hair spilling over his bare shoulders. Thoughts of kissing her haunted him. Memories of her softness, her voluptuous curves and her hands fluttering over him made him hot. She stood only a short distance away, pure temptation, and he wanted to reach for her…until he thought about all the problems between them. And it had to be a problem of some kind that brought her to see him. One glance in her big green eyes and he knew she was angry.

"Hi," he said. "What brings you here?"

Glaring at him, Emily waved papers in his face and then shoved them into his hand while she snapped, "You're welcome."

Startled out of his fantasy, Tom focused on her. "What am I welcome for? What are these papers?" he asked, looking down and turning over the official-looking forms in his hands before he looked up at her again. Puzzled, he met her fiery green eyes that flashed with fury.

"You can thank me now, because I've given you what you want—your freedom. You're free to marry the mother of your children."

"What the hell are you talking about?" She was rarely in a rage, but he could see she was boiling.

"Your secret is out, Tom," she said, her voice quivering with wrath. "You hid your family well.

Have you paid Maverick to keep your secret? Or
has it already spread all over Royal?"

Mystified, he saw that while she was shaking
with rage, she was also fighting to hold back tears.
"What the hell are you talking about, and what
are these papers? And why are you talking about
Maverick? What do you know about Maverick?"

"I think you know the answers to some of those
questions," she said in a tight voice. "You have
your divorce papers. You'll be free to be with your
other wife."

"Other wife?" Stunned, Tom repeated the words
as he frowned. "Emily, what are you talking about?
There is no other wife—"

"Oh, please. I have proof. I've seen the picture
of you and your family." She started to turn away.

Tom reached out to take her arm. As she yanked
free of his grasp, the pain of her rejection made
him hurt from head to toe. In three long strides, he
caught up with her and held her arm more tightly
this time.

"Emily, I don't understand what you're talking
about. Mother of my children? You're not leaving
until you tell me what's going on."

"You can drop the lies and false front now that
I know the truth," she snapped, twisting away to
head back to her car.

Shocked, he went after her again with long
strides that closed the distance between them. He

grasped her shoulder to turn her to face him. "I have no idea what you're talking about or what brought this divorce on so suddenly without us talking about it."

"We're through and you know it. Your other family is what brought it on. I got an email from Maverick about them." She yanked free from him again and turned to open her car door.

He closed her door and stepped between her and the car. In minutes she would be gone and he wouldn't have any answers. He placed his hand on her shoulder. "You can't pop in and tell me we're getting divorced and then leave. Tell me what the hell all this is. And tell me about this email from Maverick. That troll who's blackmailing people in town? When did you get that?"

She twisted free again. "Get out of my way."

"Like hell I will. You're not going until you tell me. There is no secret family. That's nonsense."

"Oh, no? Tom, how could you be so deceitful?" she asked, sneering at him as she fumbled in a pocket to pull out a wrinkled piece of paper and wave it in front of him. "Here's proof, Tom. Here's your picture with your family. You have your arm around your secret wife. How could you lie to me like this?" Tears filled Emily's eyes, her cheeks were red and her voice was tight with anger. "How could you do this?" she repeated. "You've hurt me again, but this will be the last time."

"Give me that," he said, taking the paper from her to smooth it out and look at it. As he did, she wiggled away and opened her car door.

Determined to get answers from her, Tom reached out to push the car door closed again, stepping close with his hip against the door so she couldn't get inside while he smoothed the paper more to look at it. "Don't go anywhere, Emily, until we get this straightened out."

"Don't you dare tell me what to do," she said in a low voice that was filled with rage.

He paid no attention to her as he focused on the computer printout. Startled, Tom realized it was a copy of a very familiar snapshot.

Two

"Emily," he said, his anger changing to curiosity, "you got this in an email? This is Natalie Valentine and her kids. She's Jeremy Valentine's widow, who owns the Cimarron Rose Bed-and-Breakfast. Why have you filed for divorce over Natalie Valentine?"

Wide-eyed, Emily looked up at Tom and then glanced at the picture. "Jeremy Valentine?" she repeated, sounding dazed. "That's his wife? You told me about his death."

"That's right. I told you how he died on a mission and my promise to him to take care of his family if he didn't make it back."

"I remember that," Emily said, sounding stunned

and confused. "She looked vaguely familiar, but I was in so much shock, I just didn't put anything together." She sagged against the car.

"Jeremy was shot," Tom reminded her. "We were on a mission in Iraq to rescue three hostages and Jeremy was shot twice. I promised him if he didn't make it, I'd take care of his family," Tom said, momentarily lost in remembering the battle, the blood, the noise of guns and men yelling. Tom looked at Emily, who had grown pale. Her eyes no longer held anger but uncertainty; he was sure she remembered him telling her about Jeremy's death.

"He was so worried about his family because he didn't expect to make it. I told him I'd be there for them if he couldn't." Tom held out the picture. "This is Natalie, and she's doing a great job being brave and upbeat and pouring herself into taking care of their two kids."

"Heavens, Tom," Emily whispered, shaking her head. "Those kids are Jeremy Valentine's? I've made a terrible mistake."

"Jeremy was their dad. They're really sweet kids. Colby is four—just like our Ryan when we lost him. Colby has autism. He's gotten accustomed to me and he's pretty relaxed around me. Lexie is two and thinks she's seventeen. She's pretty and cute. I just try to help out, because there's always something that needs fixing at the B and B. I try to be a man in the kids' lives and do things around the place or with the kids that Jeremy would do. Jeremy was one of the best."

Emily focused on him with a piercing look. "Tom, have you slept with Natalie?"

"Never," he answered with a clear conscience. "That isn't what this is about. I'm helping Natalie out, for Jeremy. That's all there is to it. He was a buddy and he died for his country." Tom gazed into Emily's green eyes and wondered whether she believed him or not. "It would be a good idea if you two met. Natalie has a sweet family."

"Oh, Tom," Emily said. She looked as if she'd been punched in the gut. Her shoulders sagged and she frowned. She ran her hand across her brow. "I've made a big mistake then," she repeated.

"I think you did," he said quietly. "But not one that can't be fixed."

Emily nodded. "I owe you an apology, because I believed this, even though it was so unlike you. The picture really shocked me."

"Forget that. We've got this ironed out between us now as far as I'm concerned, and I'll arrange for you and Natalie to meet."

"You never told me about seeing them. If it was just to be a help and do this for Jeremy, why didn't you tell me? I could have done some things for them, too."

He felt a ripple of impatience. "You haven't been interested in anything I've done for a long time.

We don't keep up with each other any longer. I don't know any more about what you're doing than you know about what I'm doing. We're out of each other's lives now." He looked down at the papers in his hand. "This divorce was inevitable."

Clamping her lips shut, she nodded. "That's true. I can see why you didn't tell me." She frowned. "So this troll just sent the message to upset and hurt me," Emily said quietly, as if more to herself than to Tom, but he heard her.

"You got this from Maverick?"

"Yes."

"Damnation," Tom said, his temper rising as he thought about someone hiding behind a fictitious name, sending hateful messages to try to hurt Emily, who had already suffered the worst possible losses. He had failed Emily in the worst possible way before, but he wasn't going to fail her this time. "There's too much damn hate in this world and we don't need this going on in Royal. Maverick." He said the name with distaste. "Someone has hurt you once, but I damn well can see that he doesn't hurt you again. First of all, unless you've already called him, I'm calling Nathan Battle and letting him know about this," Tom said, pulling his phone out of his pocket.

"Sheriff Battle?"

"Yes. This week it's a hateful message to you. Who knows what this might escalate into next or how much this troll might hurt someone else? For some reason, he or she or they want to hurt you or you wouldn't have received that email. But I can't imagine you have an enemy in this world."

"Frankly, Tom, I didn't think about calling the sheriff. I was thinking more about us."

"I'm glad to hear you say that. If you get another message from Maverick, call me the minute you do."

"You saw the message—it was on target," she said quietly, and his anger increased at hearing the pain in her voice.

"It was a lie meant to hurt you. I'll call Nathan right now."

Tom's anger boiled and he was frustrated not to be able to take more direct action. When Nathan answered, Tom quickly told him about the email. After a minute or two, he turned to Emily. "Nathan wants to come pick up your CPU. He knows it most likely won't do any good, but he doesn't want to overlook anything."

"I don't mind if he checks the CPU and the email," she answered. "Goodness, I have nothing to hide. I'm going back into town, so I can drop it off at his office."

Tom smiled, then went back to talking to the sheriff for a minute before ending the call. "We'll go by his office. I'll help you get your CPU."

"That's fine. How do you suppose someone got that picture? Do you remember who took it?"

"There was some guy, about seventy years old, staying at the bed-and-breakfast. He was taking pictures. I'm sure he didn't know any of us."

"Well, then, how did Maverick get the picture?"

"The guy was using a camera. Maybe he got the prints made at a store. Those can be handled by several people. It wouldn't be hard to get a copy." He tilted his head to look at her. "Do you have plans tonight?"

"Not at all," she answered.

"Good. Because I'm moving back in," Tom announced in an authoritative voice that she assumed he'd developed in the Rangers. "I want to stay close, because no one knows Maverick's ultimate intentions."

Startled, Emily stared at him. "I appreciate your offer but it's not necessary. I'm not staying on the ranch any longer. I'm going to restore Uncle Woody's house and move in there. I've put a cot in a bedroom and I'm already living in Royal."

"You've moved off the ranch?" Tom said, frowning. "Look, Maverick isn't getting the reaction from us that he, she or they expected, which will increase the hatred and anger toward you. Move back to the ranch until this Maverick gets caught. You'll be safer here."

She might have been tempted to do what he asked, except he was asking for the wrong reason. She wasn't moving back because of an email message. And now that she knew the truth and Tom still was the same Tom she had always known, she had lost her anger toward him. But they still had all the problems they'd had for the past five years. She was going to move into town and Tom wasn't going to stop her.

As she calmed down, the feelings and responses she had always had began to return, including noticing his thick black hair that was a tangle over his forehead but always looked appealing to her. She could remember running her fingers through his hair. Her gaze slid down and she thought about his strong arms holding her against his rock-hard chest.

She sighed, because the memories were a torment and she couldn't keep them from happening. The breeze caught locks of his hair and blew them slightly. Everything about him made her want to walk into his arms and hold him close. She had always thought he was good-looking, and as the years went by, he seemed more handsome than ever. Or did she feel that way just because he was more off-limits than ever? She wasn't staying on the ranch no matter what he said, because they had been too unhappy together there. There were too many bad memories in the big house on the ranch.

"I'll be fine in town," she said, knowing that was the best place for her to be. "I'm working at my studio four days a week now, and the other days, I can work on the house."

"Okay, I'll get a sleeping bag and stay with you in Royal. You don't know if you're in any danger from this troll. Just because nothing's happened in the past doesn't mean it won't in the future."

Startled, she stared at him. "You can't live in Royal—you have a ranch to run," she blurted, feeling a sudden panic that they would be in close quarters. No matter what problems they had, when they were together, the physical attraction was impossible to resist. She had been trying to get over him and build a new life. If they lived together, she wouldn't be able to resist him.

"You don't need to spend all that time driving back and forth every day from Royal to the ranch," she said. She was pleased that he was concerned and had made the offer, and overwhelmingly relieved to discover that the troll's message hadn't been true and Tom was still the same trustworthy person she had always thought he was, but her panic about spending nights under the same roof again began to revive. She gazed into his thickly lashed hazel eyes, which made her get a tightness low inside and think about his kisses that could melt her.

"If you're in danger and something happened

to you in Royal while I'm out here on the ranch," he said, "I couldn't live with it. You'd do the same if the situation were reversed."

She had to smile at the thought of being a bodyguard for Tom. "That's such a stretch of the imagination, I can't picture it. Don't even think about moving to Royal, but thank you for the offer, which is nice of you," she said, running her fingers along his forearm, feeling the solid muscles. She had meant it as a friendly gesture of gratitude, but the minute her fingers touched his arm, a sizzling current spiraled in her and she thought again of having his strong arms around her.

As she drew a deep breath, she saw his eyes narrow. Either he felt something, too, or he knew that she had—or both.

She dropped her hand instantly and stepped back. "Thanks anyway," she said, dismissing his offer.

"Give some thought to this. For all we know, you might be in danger. The safest possible place would be in the guesthouse. I can protect you the easiest there."

"I don't think that's necessary at all. According to the rumors I've heard, Maverick hasn't done anything except send terrible messages, trying to blackmail Royal citizens and stir up trouble. I need to work in town and I don't want to drive back and forth. I'm staying at my uncle's. Thank you for your concern, but you don't need to stay with me," she said firmly.

"I've already lost one of the most important people in my life," he said in a tight voice. "I don't intend to let anything happen to you." His hazel eyes looked darker, as they did when he was emotional or making love. "I'm going to ask Nathan to have someone drive by Natalie's and check on her to make sure she and her family are protected and okay." Tom removed his phone from his pocket again. Emily wondered who he was calling now until she heard him say hello to their foreman.

"Hey, Gus. I need to be away from the ranch for a while."

Even as she stepped in front of him and shook her head, trying to discourage him, she knew the futility of her efforts. Tom had made up his mind that she should have protection and she wouldn't be able to stop him. She threw up her hands and walked away as he gave instructions to Gus. How was she going to be able to resist Tom if they were under the same roof? Maybe he would stay downstairs and she could stay upstairs, or vice versa.

"There, now," he said when he finished talking to the foreman. "I'll bring my sleeping bag and stay in the old house with you. I won't be in your way, and I can help you with the restoration."

Exasperated, she stared at him. While she was annoyed, she knew this alpha male attitude was part of why she had been drawn to him in the first place. He was decisive and got things done. In high school it had been part of his appeal. Now she was glad he could make a decision and solve problems, but this time she really didn't want him interfering in her life by taking charge. Each time she thought about being back under the same roof with him all night, her heart pounded. If he was going to help with the restoration of the old house, they would be working together. And she couldn't trust her physical response to Tom. He would stir up all those latent longings again. Tom had a virile, sexy body. He was superbly fit from the Rangers and from ranch work.

Tom turned to her. He had his hands on his hips and he stood close. He had the shadow of stubble on his face and his tangled hair added to his disheveled attraction. He looked more appealing than ever in a rugged, sexy way. She realized where her thoughts were drifting and tried to pay attention to what he was saying.

"Nathan told me that Case Baxter, president of the TCC, plans to have an emergency meeting this coming week. Case agrees with Nathan that Maverick has to be stopped. To do so, they need to learn Maverick's true identity. I'm going to that meeting, and I'd like you to come with me."

"Sure, I'll go. But I don't think I can help in any way."

"It won't hurt, and the more of us who are informed and keep in touch with Nathan, the more likely he'll be able to catch Maverick. If you go, remember, Maverick may be sitting in the audience."

She shivered. "That's creepy."

"Hopefully, his emails and threats on social media won't escalate into violence, but no one knows right now. What he's doing now is bad enough. He hasn't really hurt us, but he could have, and he can hurt others badly."

After a pause, Emily steered the conversation to an equally unpleasant topic. "Tom, when we've waited a bit, we need to sit down and talk about the divorce and how we'll divide things. I was so angry when I filed. The picture was so convincing."

He nodded. "I don't think we'll have a problem dividing up the ranch, the house, the cars or the plane."

"You can definitely have the plane," she remarked, and he gave her a fleeting smile that made her smile in turn.

"I'll sign the divorce papers. We're there anyway, and you can have a life."

She turned away before he saw tears in her eyes. He was right. They were as good as divorced now, and she couldn't give him children. Their marriage had such devastating memories. Even so, it still hurt when divorce became reality; she had filed and the papers were in his possession. It was one more big loss in her life and this one she took responsibility for because she'd been unable to get pregnant again. If she had been, it would have held them together. She'd wanted so badly to give Tom another child like Ryan. There was adoption—Tom had been willing—but it wasn't the same and she was against it. She wanted to have another child like Ryan.

Now she and Tom were estranged, and if they got divorced, they could each go ahead with life. But it was difficult to imagine ever loving another man.

And it didn't help that Tom had proved Maverick wrong and was trying to help her. It was easy to file for divorce when she was so angry with Tom because she thought he had deceived her. To know that he was still the same guy she had always admired and trusted made the divorce hurt.

"Emily?"

She blinked in surprise, turning to face him again. His eyes narrowed, and he studied her intently. "I'm sorry, Tom. My thoughts drifted back to Maverick," she said, her cheeks burning with embarrassment. She suspected he could guess exactly why she hadn't heard him.

"You said you're going back to Royal from here. Let me grab a sleeping bag and a few things. I'll take you."

She opened her mouth to protest, but before she said a word, he waved his hand. "I'm taking you to Royal. Tomorrow we'll come back and get your car. I'd just as soon let everyone see us together—it'll give me pleasure. Hopefully, the damned troll will see us and realize that email did no harm. Far from it. How's that for a plan?"

She shrugged. "I have a feeling if I didn't like it at all, I would still end up doing it. I think you're right about letting Maverick see us together. That gives me a sense of getting even with the troll."

"We can flaunt that we're getting along. It doesn't take long for word to get around Royal."

"I agree. While it's good to be seen together, you don't need to stay with me," she argued again. "I'll be in town, where I can call for help at any hour and someone will be right there."

"I'm staying, Emily. This is someone with a grudge and you're on the list. That was a damn hateful message you received. Look at the results. You filed for divorce. If rumors started, they could have hurt Natalie, which in turn would have hurt her kids. Frankly, I'm not ready to divorce you when it's because of a bunch of lies from a vengeful creep."

"You have a point, Tom," she said, wishing he had said he didn't want the divorce for other reasons, yet knowing he was right. "And while we've been talking, I've been thinking—Maverick has to be somebody who lives in Royal, or has lived in Royal until recently, to know this about you and Natalie and to know to send the picture to me."

"That's right." He looked down at his dusty boots, his mud-splattered jeans. "Can you have a seat inside and let me take a quick shower? I can be speedy."

"You were never speedy when I showered with you," she teased and then blushed. "I don't know where that came from," she said. "Forget it."

"Hell, no, I won't forget it," he said, his voice getting soft. "You were teasing like you used to, and that's allowed, Emily. We can have some fun sometimes—let it happen. We've got too much of the sad stuff. At this point in our lives, it really isn't going to change anything to have a laugh or two," he said.

She nodded. "I suppose you're right," she said quietly, thinking he was the way he used to be before the bad times set in. Relaxed, kind, understanding, practical, sexy. He had been fun, so much fun, so sexy. She waved her hand at him. "Go on, Tom. Shower. I can go get the CPU while you're in there."

"Nope. I want to be with you. This Maverick bothers me, I'll admit. I can't imagine why you're on anyone's hit list. That's worrisome. You're soft-hearted, generous—"

"Oh, my! We've turned into a mutual-admiration society, thanks to a troll."

"It's not thanks to the damned troll. It's time we have something between us again that isn't sad, even if it's just for five minutes."

"Tom, I agree with everything you just said. For just a few minutes, it was sort of the way it used to be, at least a tiny bit," she said, suddenly serious, thinking it was a lot better than not speaking and avoiding each other. "I know we can't turn back the clock, but we can at least be civil to each other."

"Damn right. Don't disappear while I go shower," he said, starting inside and holding the screen door. He paused, looking over his shoulder at her. "Unless you want to come inside and join me."

She shook her head. "No, thank you."

He grinned. "After your remark, I had to try." He let the door slam shut behind him and disappeared.

"Don't make me fall in love with you all over again," she whispered, and wound her fingers together, trying to think of seeing Nathan Battle, of her appointments tomorrow, of anything except Tom in the shower.

In less than ten minutes Tom reappeared, his hair slightly damp. He wore a clean navy T-shirt, fresh jeans, black boots and a black hat. He carried a rolled-up sleeping bag and a satchel. "I'll put up my truck and get the car and we'll go get the CPU."

"Sure," she said, walking out with him and waiting on the porch until he pulled up in a black sports car. He was out and around the car by the time she got to it. He held the door for her, and as she passed him, she glanced up and received another scalding look. She was close, her shoulder brushing his arm as he held the car door open. Their gazes met and she couldn't catch her breath. For just a moment, she forgot everything except Tom, pausing to look into his thickly lashed hazel eyes that immobilized her. The differences between them fell away, and all-consuming lust enveloped her.

It took an effort to tear her gaze from his. In that brief moment, she had wanted his arms around her and his mouth on hers.

"Thanks," she said, hating that it came out breathlessly. She slipped into the passenger seat and gazed ahead as he closed the door. He strode around the car. Handsome, purposeful, filled with vitality, he would be married again after their divorce, she was certain. Tom was too appealing to live alone, and he liked women. The idea of Tom marrying hurt even though they had no future together and no longer had the joy and happiness of their first years together.

She rode in silence as they drove the short distance from the guesthouse to the mansion they had shared. Now it stood silent and empty. They had been happy in the sprawling, palatial two-story house until they lost their son. She didn't want to live in it alone. It was too big, too empty without Tom. He'd seemed to fill it with his presence when he would come home. When they had Ryan, his childish voice and laughter had also seemed to fill the big house. At present, she found it empty, isolated and sad. She didn't like living alone in it and she didn't intend to ever again. This wasn't the place for her any longer.

The house had a somber effect on her and Tom seemed to react the same way. They both were quiet as they walked to the door. Tom still had a key and opened the door to hold it for her. She walked through into the spacious entryway, switching on lights as she went, although it wasn't dark outside yet.

She suddenly thought about Ryan running around in front of the house when he was so small. Tears came and she wiped them away quickly. Pausing, she glanced over her shoulder at Tom, and he looked stricken. She guessed that he, too, was thinking of Ryan and hurting because he hadn't been in the house in almost a year. He rubbed his eyes—the tough, decorated Ranger who had been in combat, been wounded, been a prisoner until he escaped. She couldn't bear his grief, which compounded her pain. When she turned away, crying silently while she tried to get control of her emotions, Tom put his arm around her.

"Come here," he whispered. Sobbing, she turned to him and they held each other. His strong arms around her felt wonderful and she tightened her hold on him as if she could squeeze out some of his strength, transferring it from him to her. He was a comfort and she hoped she was for him. She stroked his back, relishing holding him. It had been so long since she had been in his arms.

"I'm sorry, Tom. Sometimes I just lose it and I guess you do, too. Having you here helps," she said, wiping her eyes with a tissue.

He looked down at her, easing his hold on her slightly. "I'm glad I'm here for you. It helps me. Grieving is part of it that we can't escape." She nodded as he released her. She missed his strong arms around her.

"I'm okay now. Thanks."

They went through the house to the large room that was her office. "I'll get the CPU out for you, Emily," he said and strode past her. "I'm sure this is futile, but it would be ridiculous for Nathan not to check it out."

"While you do that, Tom, I'll pick up a few things to take to Royal."

"Where's that white cat of yours?"

"Your cook has Snowball until I get settled in Royal. You don't care, do you?"

"No, I don't care where your cat is."

It seemed natural to be in the house with Tom again. She watched him hunker down to disconnect the CPU, the fabric of his jeans pulling tightly over his long legs. Desire swept through her, and she turned to leave the room abruptly to get away from him.

In less than half an hour they were on their way to Royal. They rode together in silence. She knew he was bound in his own thoughts as much as she was in hers, and they had little to say to each other. While they didn't talk, she was acutely conscious of him. She hadn't been around him this much in a long time. And their time together was just starting. How could she live under the same roof with him again without being in his arms and in his bed and back on an emotional roller coaster?

She glanced at his hand on the steering wheel. He had a scar across the back of it that had healed long ago. He had scars all over his body from his time in the military.

His hands were well shaped, nails clipped very short, veins showing slightly. Too easily she could remember his hands drifting over her when they had made love—strong hands that could send her to paradise.

She realized her thoughts were carrying her into a place she didn't want to go. "I think you're right about the divorce. We'll get it—that's inevitable—

but I don't like getting a divorce because of Maverick, either."

"Let's table the divorce for now. I'll try to find out how much effort Nathan is devoting to catching this troll. The meeting Monday at the club may shed more light. If we don't divorce and we both stay at the house in Royal—"

"Maverick will know you've become my bodyguard," she said, shaking her head.

"Not necessarily. If I help you restore the old house, it'll look as if we're back together. For all anyone knows, we're fixing it up for you to sell. For a few weeks, maybe we should keep quiet that I'm worried about your protection and that we're not really together anymore."

"That's fine with me. Anything to defeat Maverick. Frankly, I'm still amazed I'm a victim. I'm not the sweetest person, but I usually get along with people I know and work with, neighbors, church friends."

"I'll ask you the question that Nathan is going to ask—do you have any enemies? Anyone who doesn't like you or you've angered?"

She laughed softly. "Tom, I may have people who don't like me, but if so, I don't know anything about it. I don't have enemies. I can't think of anyone."

"The whole world loves you," he remarked. "That's what you'll hear from Nathan, I'll bet."

"The one person I've made the most unhappy is you," she answered quietly, and he glanced quickly at her and back at the road. When she looked again, she saw his knuckles had tightened on the wheel.

"Hell, Emily, I loved you with all my being, but we've just had so much happen between us there is no way we can go back to that life we had. When I ask if you have angered anyone, I'm talking real enemies."

"I know you are," she said, hurting inside because she'd answered with the truth. There was no one who had been as hurt by her or more at odds with her or more disappointed by her than Tom. "We're not real enemies and you're a good guy."

"Thanks for that much, Em. Think about it. Think if there is anyone you've crossed who might hold a grudge."

She gave a small laugh. "Darla from our class in high school. Oh, did she have a crush on you. Now if this had happened when we were sixteen instead of now when we're thirty-two, I'd give out her name in a flash, but the last I heard she's married and has three kids."

"I hate to say this, but I don't even remember the person you're talking about."

"One of your groupies."

"I didn't have groupies."

"Every cute football captain has groupies."

"May have seemed so to you, but I didn't. And I haven't been called cute since I was five."

"You were cute. That was the general consensus with all the girls. Ooh, long eyelashes, broad shoulders, cute butt, sexy, to-die-for—"

"Stop it." He laughed. "If I had only known then—you didn't tell me all that when we were in school."

"Of course not. It would have just gone to your head—or elsewhere."

"Oh, damn, we should have had this conversation long ago," he said, grinning at her. And once again, for just an instant, she was reminded of old times with him.

"Kidding aside, Emily, keep thinking. It's important. Could it have to do with your business?"

"I take pictures of kids and families—there's nothing in my work that should anger anyone. I've never had an irate customer."

"I'm sure you haven't—you're a damn good photographer."

"The result wasn't what Maverick intended, so let's not worry too much about it right now," she said, placing her hand on Tom's knee in a gesture that at one time would have been casual. It wasn't now. He turned to stare at her, and she saw his chest expand as he took a deep breath.

She removed her hand and looked out the window, turning from him and trying to make light of the moment. She was thankful he couldn't hear or feel her racing heart.

"I'll try to think, but I'm blank. I know I'm overlooking something or I wouldn't have received that email."

"That's right, so work on it," he said, and they lapsed into silence as they drove toward Royal.

She thought over what Tom had said. What enemies did she have? "Tom, maybe Maverick was getting at you through me."

"That occurred to me, and I've been trying to think of anyone in these parts I could have really annoyed. Frankly, Emily, I can think of some. I've fired cowboys who didn't want to work. I was in the military—there are people in the area who don't like that or what I did. Politically, they don't agree with me. There are guys I competed with in college and high school sports. There are guys I've competed with in rodeos. I'll talk to Nathan about it. He's got to catch this troll. It has to be someone really low-down mean to hurt you after what you've been through."

"I haven't been through any more than you have," she said, and he was silent. His jaw was set and she suspected he was frustrated and angry.

"You have been through more than I have," he said quietly. "You lost Ryan, you lost your uncle, your dad split when you were two, your mom died when you were nine, the man who raised you and the last close member of your family died this past year and you haven't had another child. You don't need more anguish, much less to get hassled by a rotten coward."

It hurt to hear Tom say that she couldn't have more children, but everything he said was the truth. As their conversation trailed off, she was acutely aware of him so nearby. She had been doing fairly well when she didn't see him or talk to him on a regular basis, but now to be with him, to joke around with him, even just this tiny bit, drew her to him. And the memories were tormenting her. They had been so wildly in love when they were dating and first married. Her world had crashed and would never again be the same. She had been slowly adjusting to life without Tom, and now he was coming right back into it. Would she be able to cope with living in the same house again? Could she resist the intense, scalding attraction she always felt for him? What would happen if he tried to seduce her?

The questions came at her constantly, and there were no answers.

Three

When they got to town, Tom parked in front of the sheriff's office and carried the CPU inside. Nathan greeted them and shook Tom's hand. "We don't have much in the way of good leads and I don't expect to get anything from your computer, but I need to check it out. I hope both of you will go to the meeting Monday."

"We plan to," Tom said. "I'll help in any way I can. Just let me know."

"Thanks," Nathan said. The sheriff was tall and had friendly brown eyes. "I'd like to talk to each of you, one at a time. Emily, want to go first?"

"Sure," she answered, smiling at him. He was

slightly older than Tom and she, but she knew him and his wife, Amanda, who owned the Royal Diner, which was a town fixture.

Emily went into his office and tried to answer his questions. She was with him only a short time and then he talked to Tom. Their session was also brief.

Soon both men came out of Nathan's office. "If either one of you think of anything to tell me, just call, no matter what the hour is. I want this Maverick caught."

"I think most of the people in Royal probably want him caught quickly," Emily said.

"Sorry we weren't more help, Nathan," Tom said. "I'll keep thinking about any possibilities."

"Sure. Both of you try to make the meeting Monday. I'm shocked that Emily was a target. And it could have been to get at you, but why you? You don't have any real enemies around these parts."

"You never know—you can aggravate someone without even knowing it. Since there are several people now who've received these Maverick messages, I'd say this is a sour character who has a lot of grudges."

"You're right. I want to catch him—or her. I'm sure Emily's computer will be the same as the others—we can't trace where the messages originated. Maverick may be mean, but he's not stupid."

Nathan followed them outside, and the three

of them stood for a moment in the late-afternoon sun. "Emily, since you've moved into your uncle's house here in town, if you need us at any time, just call. I'm glad Tom is there now, because that takes away some worries."

"We'll keep in touch," Tom promised as he took Emily's arm lightly. He was saying goodbye to the sheriff, paying little attention to her, but with each of Tom's touches, the contact was startling. How could he still do this to her when they were no longer in love and headed for divorce? They had no future together, she was annoyed he had taken charge of her life and was staying with her, yet the slightest contact was electrifying. She hoped her reaction didn't show.

They told Nathan goodbye and walked to the car. As they drove away, Tom glanced at her. "Let's stop at the diner and get a burger."

"Sure," she answered, knowing Tom was probably hungry, but suspecting he wanted people in Royal to see them together.

Everything they did reminded her of old times with him, which made her sad, but at the same time, she couldn't keep from enjoying his company.

They drove the short distance down Main and stopped at the Royal Diner for burgers. Too many things she did with Tom reminded her of their life when everything was exciting and they were in love. The reminders hurt and made her realize how her expectations had been destroyed and there wasn't any putting their marriage back together. They might fool Maverick, but it was going to cost her peace of mind to have Tom hovering around.

They sat down in a booth upholstered in red faux leather. "How many times have we eaten burgers or had a malt here?" she couldn't resist asking Tom.

He smiled at her. "Too many to keep track, but my mind was never on the burgers or the malts."

"I doubt mine was, either," she said, remembering how exciting he was to her. "This is the first place you asked me to go with you—to get a malt."

"I remember," he said, focusing on her with a direct gaze that made her warm. "After you ran into my car."

"That was one of the first times I ever took the car. I just didn't see you when I pulled out of the school parking lot. It's a good thing you had quick reflexes, because it would have been a worse wreck if you hadn't put on your brakes."

"That seems so long ago. Your uncle Woody was understanding about the whole thing. His insurance paid for my car and he had faith in you. He knew you'd learn to drive, and I guess he figured you'd be more careful after hitting my car."

"I was definitely more careful."

"It was worth it to get you to pick me up every

morning and take me to school while my car was being fixed," Tom said, smiling at her.

"I thought so, too," she said, loving to see him smile. The sad times they'd experienced had taken away smiles and laughter, but before that she had always had more fun with Tom than anyone else. "I liked picking you up, except it was embarrassing, too, because everyone in school knew what I'd done."

He leaned across the table, and his voice dropped as he spoke softly. "Remember our first kiss? I do."

She looked into his bedroom eyes and drew a deep breath. But it felt as if all the air in the diner suddenly vanished. She couldn't keep from glancing at Tom's mouth, thinking about his kisses, remembering them in exacting detail and wanting to kiss him again.

"Of course I do, but I'm surprised you do."

"I do. Why do you think I asked you out again?" he said, those hazel eyes twinkling.

"It was all exciting, Tom," she said, full of regret.

"Then don't cry about it now. Happy memories. Take the ones that were special and exciting and concentrate on them."

"Thank you, Doctor," she said lightly, smiling at him.

Their burgers came. She ate half of hers, reflecting on how she didn't want Tom staying with her but finding no way to avoid it, especially after Nathan said it was a good arrangement.

They left and she felt certain they would never eat burgers together in the Royal Diner again. She glanced up at Tom as she walked beside him. He was still exciting to her, which was something she didn't want to feel, because they had no future and all too soon they would officially be divorced. Why did that hurt so badly when it was what they both wanted? Now with him moving in to stay in the same house with her, was she going through another emotional upheaval that would be more difficult and painful to get over than the last time?

"Want to make a quick stop and see my studio?" she asked impulsively. "It isn't something you have to do."

"No, I'd like to see it."

"Turn at the next corner." She gave him directions and they drove just two more blocks and parked in front. She was sandwiched in between a law office and a popular bakery that had delicious bread. He paused to look at the pictures of babies and dogs and families on display in her front window.

"Very nice, Em. You've turned your hobby into a good business. You're very good."

"Thank you," she said, feeling he was being polite.

"I think I may just stand out here and smell the bread," Tom remarked.

"It's fantastic. We can pick up a loaf to take with us. They have specialties. Come in. This is tiny, but big enough for me."

He walked around the waiting room, looking at more pictures on the walls. Some of the people he recognized, a lot he didn't, especially the children. Then he came upon a large framed picture of their son when he was two years old.

"Em, this is a wonderful picture of Ryan. I want a copy."

"I'll get you one. I'm glad you like it. It makes me happy to see his picture when I come to work."

Tom continued looking at the framed photographs. There was one from when the tornado hit Royal, of the damaged town hall with three floors destroyed and the clock tower left standing. "You're very good at this," he said, moving to another picture of a black horse in a pasture, the wind blowing its tail, sunlight spilling over its satiny black coat. Tom glanced at her.

"This looks like my horse Grand."

"It is. He's photogenic and cooperative."

"Wow. I'd like a copy of that picture, too." He leaned closer. "I don't see a price on these."

"You're special. You can have that picture compliments of the house."

"You don't need to do that."

"I want to," she said, smiling at him.

"Thanks. It's a great picture of him."

"Come see where I take pictures and my desk."

He walked around and bent down to look through a camera set on a tripod. Across from him was a backdrop of a field of green grass.

"Tom, let me take your picture."

He grinned at her. "You're kidding. You know what I look like."

She took his arm. "Come stand and let me have a picture of you. I might want it on cold winter nights when you're not with me."

His smile faded. "You're serious. All right, I will if you'll let me take one of you on my phone."

She laughed. "Sure I will."

"And promise you won't stick me out there in the window."

"I wouldn't think of it," she said. "Your picture will go home to my bedroom," she said, expecting a laugh or sexy reply, but he stood quietly looking at her and she wondered what he was thinking. "You stand right here," she said, motioning to him.

Behind the camera, she adjusted the settings and took a picture. "Now turn slightly and look over your shoulder a little at me and smile."

"Em, I feel silly."

"Smile and cooperate. I'll buy you a loaf of bread when we leave."

"You're really good at this bribery business." He turned and smiled and she snapped some more.

"Now, want to see your pictures? I can get proofs for you while we go get that loaf of bread."

"I don't really care about seeing my picture, but I definitely care about that bread. You don't have to buy it. I'll go get it and you get your proofs or whatever you do. What kind do you want me to get?"

"I love the sourdough."

"Sourdough, coming up. I'll be back." He left and she worked quickly on the proof. She was examining them when she heard the bell in front. She scooped up the proofs, turned off lights and hurried to meet him.

"I have two loaves of bread and they smell almost too good to wait to eat. Ready to go?"

"Yes, look. You take a very appealing picture."

She held a couple of proofs out for him to see. He barely glanced at them but smiled at her. "I'm a very appealing subject," he said and she smiled.

The sun was low in the west when they left her shop. As soon as they were in the car, she turned to him slightly. "When we leave here, get ready for a shock. The house is in terrible condition. At the last, Uncle Woody was so ill—"

"Emily, I've meant to tell you that I'm sorry I missed being at his funeral."

"There wasn't any reason for you to fly back from your business trip in Wyoming. I never asked you if you bought the ranch," she said, realizing how far apart they had grown. In times past he would have been at her side for her uncle's last hours and through the service. She would have known whether Tom bought another ranch in Wyoming and he would have discussed his decision with her before he did anything. They were moving farther apart and the divorce was inevitable, but right now, she didn't want to give any satisfaction to Maverick and neither did Tom, so they'd stay together.

"No, I didn't buy it. If I buy another ranch, it'll be in this part of the country," he said. "I'm beginning to rethink getting someone else to run it. I have to be hands-on with a ranch."

She was quiet when they turned on the street where she had lived from the time she was nine years old until she had married Tom. Big sycamores and oaks lined the road. Tiny green leaves covered some branches, but many had bare limbs. The aging sidewalk was pushed up by tree roots. Tom slowed in front of the three-story house and turned onto a driveway where grass filled the cracks of aged concrete that had disappeared beneath a cover of weeds.

Tom parked beside the back corner of the aged house. "I want the car out here where it can be seen. If anyone has been watching you, whoever it is will know this isn't your car. I want Maverick to know I'm here with you, that the email didn't work and didn't hurt either one of us."

"It gives me the shivers to think someone might be watching me," she said. "I never even thought of that."

Tom gave her a look and smiled. "You're trusting."

He cut the engine while he gazed at the house, and she studied it with him. Long ago it had been painted white, but now the paint was peeling. There were gables on the front and west sides with a shingled roof that needed replacement. The large round tower on the east side had broken windows and all the ground floor windows were broken. The house had a wraparound porch with wooden gingerbread decoration that had shattered through the years and ornate spindles that were broken.

She sat a moment looking at the dilapidated condition: peeling paint, shutters hanging awry or gone, broken windows, concrete steps crumbling. She remembered one night when Tom had brought her home and parked on the drive. They had gotten out of his car and he had kissed her beneath the mulberry tree. A kiss became kisses and then he asked her to marry him. They both had a year of college left and they'd talked about waiting, but that night was the night he proposed. Before she went in, they agreed they wouldn't do anything official until they finished their senior year.

"What are you thinking about?" he asked.

Startled, she turned to him and wondered if he had guessed that being with him at the house had triggered memories. "I have a lot of windows to repair," she said.

"Yeah," he said in a gruff voice, and she wondered if he remembered the same moments she had. "So this is where you want to live instead of the house on the ranch. This is going to be a job and a half," Tom said, looking at it in the dusk as the last sunlight slipped away into darkness. "It's also the least secure place you could pick to stay."

"I'm in Royal, which is a peaceful town."

"A peaceful town that has a hateful troll spreading grief."

"I know I have a lot of work to do here, but I work in town now and the house is my only tie to my past and my family. The ones I was really close to are all gone. I hardly know my cousins, and they live in Oregon and Vermont. I never see them. This house is my tie to Mom and Uncle Woody."

"It's a fine old home, but your uncle couldn't keep up with it and it'll be an expense for you."

"He didn't want me to hire anyone to work on it, so I did what he wanted."

"Honoring his wishes was probably more important. Well, we can fix it up and hire people to do some of the work."

"It's not a *we* thing, Tom. This isn't where you'll

live. It's not your house and it's not your problem," she said. "You don't need to be concerned with it, and I still think you could go back to the ranch."

He frowned, his jaw clamped shut. The happy moments they'd had disappeared with her request for him to leave. Jolted by regret, she reminded herself it was for the best. She didn't need Tom staying with her, and it would complicate both their lives—he had a ranch to run and she didn't need him hovering.

"People will have seen us together and your car here and they'll talk about it. You don't need to stay longer," she added when he didn't say anything.

"You may not want me, but I'm staying," he said in a gruff tone. "Think of me as a bodyguard and maybe you can tolerate my presence. You might need me."

"Suit yourself," she said, still wondering how she would get through the night with him in the house.

She reached for the door handle and he placed his hand on hers.

Startled, she looked up at him.

"I don't feel right about you walking into this big empty house. Anybody could be in there, because there is not one lick of security here. They could step in through any one of downstairs windows. Do you even lock the doors?"

"Actually, no. What's the point with windows broken out?"

"You just wait here in the car while I check the place. Keep the car keys and give me your house key."

"Tom—"

"I know I'm being cautious, but it only takes minutes and we have time. I'll feel better. Now you stay locked in this car, and if you see anyone call me instantly. And if anyone tries to get in the car—"

"I'll just run over them," she couldn't resist saying, because she thought he was being ridiculous.

He didn't laugh. "Emily, I've seen a guy walk into a house and get his throat slashed. I know we're in Royal, but I don't see one damn reason to take a chance."

"Ah, Tom. Sorry," she said. "I know you're trying to help, but this isn't a war zone, it's Royal, and so far, Maverick has only sent emails." She waved her hand. "I'll do as you say. You check out the house." She knew his warrior background had kicked in and there was no use arguing.

Nodding at her, he stepped out of the car and closed the door quietly.

She couldn't imagine any danger, but then she had never expected to receive such a hateful message from Maverick, either. And so now she was under the same roof with Tom again—that seemed the biggest threat, but it was a threat to her heart when she was just pulling herself together and beginning to establish a life without Tom in it.

He vanished into the house. It was still dusk. She could still see outside, but inside the old house, darkness would prevail. She could imagine Tom checking out each room. He would be thorough and silent.

Her nerves were on edge by the time the lights were switched on in the house and she could see him coming through the kitchen. As she took in his broad shoulders and purposeful stride, she knew she would feel totally safe with Tom in the house. In the past she had always felt completely safe when he was around, but then, in the past, she hadn't worried about any kind of threat.

He passed by the windows and a light went off in what Uncle Woody called his front parlor. Next the hall light went off and she realized Tom was going to turn off all the lights and leave the downstairs in darkness.

She didn't even see him coming when he tapped on the car window.

He opened the door for her, pushing a button to keep the car light off. "Thanks for humoring me. I feel better about the house now." She stepped out and closed the door. He reached to help her, taking her arm. It was casual, something he obviously wasn't thinking about, but like any physical contact with him, she was intensely aware of his touch.

"Emily, you have no security here. You don't have one damn window covering except in a bathroom downstairs, and anyone watching can see where you are in the house at any time. We've got some work ahead of us. Do you have curtains or sheets here?"

"I have sheets."

"Okay, come on. Let's get moving. We need some windows covered, and you need to move upstairs."

"I don't suppose there is any point in arguing with you about moving upstairs."

"No, there isn't," he said. "That's what you're going to do."

"When did you get so take-charge?"

"When someone threatened you. You're on that troll's hit list, and until he or she is caught, don't forget that for a moment. You've crossed someone in some way and they want to get even. It could be me they're after, but if it is, that's a damn roundabout way to get at me. Just remember someone wants to hurt you."

"I don't think you're going to let me forget it."

They walked around to the back door and entered the dark house. Night had fallen and there was no moon. She realized he hadn't left any lights on in the back hall entrance.

Tom took her arm and, again, the minute his fingers touched her, she had the usual tingles from head to toe. How would she live with him in the same house, work with him to restore it? How would she get through this one night? She was always attracted to him, but she needed to resist him now. She couldn't bear to go through all the emotional upheaval she had in the past. There were no solutions to their problems, and their divorce would be finalized as soon as this threat from Maverick ended.

"Tom—"

In little more than a whisper, his breath warm on her ear, he said, "Wait until we're upstairs."

Four

They moved silently in the dark through the back hall into the breakfast room and then the main hall. When they stopped for a second, Emily collided with him.

Tom slipped his arm around her waist. The minute he did, everything changed. He became aware of her softness, the faint trace of perfume, her hair spilling across his hand. He held her lightly. Her soft blue sweater fit snugly and he could feel her warmth, her lush curves, her soft breasts pressing against his arm. Desire was sudden and intense.

Off balance, she grabbed his arm, but he held her and she wasn't going to fall. It took an effort to hold her lightly, to keep from wrapping his arms around her and kissing her until she responded. She was soft, alluring, warm.

Time disappeared and took along with it memories of the bad times and the loss. At the moment memories of holding her and kissing her consumed him, making his heart race. He tightened his arms to pull her close, feeling her slender arm slide around his neck.

"Some things between us haven't changed," he said quietly. He shifted, fitting her against him, still holding her close. The pounding beat of his heart was loud and he fought to keep control. Even though he knew the trouble it would cause, he wanted to hold her, to kiss her, to make love to her all night long.

"We can't do this, Tom," she whispered.

He couldn't answer. He was hot, hard and he wanted her. It was physical, a hungry need because he had been alone so long. He had to let her go and get upstairs, but he didn't want to release her. It had been so damned long since he had held her, kissed her or even just touched her.

He released her slightly, still holding her arm. "Are you okay?"

"Yes, I'm fine. I just stumbled," she answered. She sounded breathless and tense, and that just added to his desire. He tried to focus on the situation and stop thinking about kissing her.

"I don't want to turn on a light. You have all these damn windows. With your sunroom, you have thirty-two windows downstairs that are not covered, and anyone looking in can see what you're doing. Let's take this gear upstairs."

"I know this house even in the dark," she said. They talked in quieter tones, but he wasn't sure he was making sense, because all he could think about was kissing her. He was already tied in knots over her. Even while they talked, he continued to hold her arm and she had hers on his shoulder.

"I'm glad you know this house. We won't have to turn on lights until we're upstairs. Can you get up the steps in the dark?" he asked.

She leaned closer to his ear, her breath warm on his neck. "How many times do you think I turned out all the lights downstairs and tiptoed upstairs in total darkness after you brought me home from a date later than I was supposed to stay out? I can't recall you worrying then whether I could get up the steps in the dark."

Her words eased some of his tension and he chuckled softly. "Okay, you go ahead and I'll follow."

Reluctantly, he released her. Today, there had been moments when tension fell away. It was the way things used to be. This was a bubble in their lives—when they could live together again while

Nathan and others tried to discover Maverick's identity.

Tom stayed right behind her as she silently went up the steps in the dark, leading him to a large bedroom at the back of the house. "We're in my room, Tom. I'm going to turn a light on now."

"Go ahead. I've checked out the house and we're the only ones in it. I've been in the attic and basement. No wonder these old houses are in scary movies. Plunk one of these in a scene and you already have atmosphere before you even start."

"I love this old house and there isn't anything scary about it, including the basement."

"I'm glad to hear you say that. Let's start hanging sheets and get you some privacy. Tomorrow you buy whatever you want—shutters, shades, curtains. Get something that will be easier to deal with than sheets on the windows for these upstairs rooms. Downstairs we can hang sheets and leave them."

Lost in thoughts about Emily, Tom worked fast. He was tall enough to hang sheets in front of a lot of windows without getting on a ladder, but he needed a stepladder for others.

"This place doesn't have an alarm system. You should go ahead and get one tomorrow and make arrangements to have it installed as soon as possible. I can recommend a good one. The guy who has the franchise is an ex-Ranger and a friend. He'll do a rush job."

"You're getting really bossy," she said. Her voice was light and he knew she was teasing.

Tom got hot working, so he yanked off his shirt. When he turned around to reach for another sheet, he glanced at Emily. She stood transfixed as her gaze danced over his chest. Her cheeks were pink, her breathing fast, and desire filled her expression as she stared at him. She looked up and met his gaze, making his pulse speed up.

Without breaking eye contact, he crossed the room to her. The temperature in the room climbed and memories tugged at him—of holding her, of kissing her, of making love. Desire intensified as he looked down into her green eyes. He slipped his hand behind her head, feeling her soft hair, looking at her mouth. Memories tore at him of kissing her and how soft her mouth was. She looked up at him with a dazed expression as she shook her head.

"No," she whispered. "Tom, I was just getting adjusted to being on my own—I don't want to do this."

He could barely hear her over his pounding heart. "The hell you don't." His voice was low and gruff. "Emily, it's been so long. A kiss won't change anything. We can kiss and walk away." He was fighting to control desire because he wanted her more than he had dreamed possible. He hadn't made love to her in so long and there had been no other women. He was hard, ready, with visions taunting him of Emily naked in his arms. Memories poured over him of how she responded, of her scalding kisses and her hungry zest for making love.

He pulled her to him and kissed her passionately, wanting to take her now, hard and fast, yet knowing when she agreed to sex, he should take his time. And he felt she would agree. One look into her big green eyes and he could tell she was as ready as he was. Maybe not tonight, but soon, so soon. Heat filled him at the thought.

He bent over her and continued the kiss, dimly aware that her arms were wrapped around him and she held him tightly, rubbing against him, moaning with pleasure.

She was soft, warm, luscious in his arms. He slipped his hand over her breast and felt he would burst with hungry need to just take her now. Fighting for control, he caressed her. Her softness sent his temperature soaring. She wriggled out of his embrace and stepped back, gulping air.

"I can't do this. I just can't. It's emotional turmoil and I get too worked up and torn up. We're not good for each other. We're getting divorced."

He turned away, trying to control his desire and emotions. She wanted him out of her life. "I'll be downstairs," he said, yanking on his shirt and leaving the room, knowing he had to get that divorce and move on, let go of Emily because he made her unhappy.

He went down the steps, moving quietly, his gaze adjusting to the darkness as he reached the first floor. He looked over his shoulder and saw the light in the hall that spilled from her upstairs bedroom. She had been right—how were they going to stay in the same house, live together and not constantly hurt each other?

He wanted her, but the damned attraction between them that had been so exciting, sexy and fantastic in the early years was now an albatross for both of them.

Yet he had to stay with her. He couldn't walk out of here and leave her alone in this big rambling house that came straight out of a horror movie. She had zero security. She might not want him here any more than she had in the big house on the ranch, but he had to stay until she repaired the windows and installed alarms. Maverick scared him. What could either of them have possibly done to make someone so angry?

Tom stepped outside, letting his eyes adjust to the dark. Was anyone watching Emily? Was she in any danger?

He looked up at the house. The second story in front was as dark as the downstairs. Tom walked back to the porch and sat in the dark, trying to cool down, to stop thinking about her kiss or how soft she was. To stop thinking about divorcing Emily. It still seemed impossible.

He remembered that night on the bus in Colorado. They'd spent the day on the ski slopes near a new lodge with an indoor water park. By the time they started back to the hotel where they were staying, the weather had changed and the driver said they would skip the planned stop for dinner. In a short time, it had turned into a blizzard.

On a curve on the side of a mountain, the bus hit ice and slid off the road. Going down the mountainside, the bus crashed into trees and then rolled. Seat belts gave way and people and belongings were tossed into the aisle. The sounds of screams, yelling and crying rose above the howling wind. Emily had screamed to him to get Ryan. He wanted to protect both of them, but she was right that he had to focus on trying to help their son. Tom had tried to hold Ryan in his seat and protect him as the bus crashed down the mountain. Ryan kept crying, "Daddy! Daddy!" until his screams went silent.

Something had struck Tom, causing pain to shoot across his shoulder and arm as the bus slid on one side. Another blow brought oblivion. Seconds— or minutes—later, he'd come to and fought to stay conscious. The headlights were still on and Tom had seen a sheet of gray ice illuminated in the bus's headlights and fading into darkness—and he'd realized the momentum was carrying the bus to a frozen pond.

To Tom's horror, Ryan and the seat he had been buckled into were gone. "Ryan!" Tom's shout had been lost in all the chaos and noise. His cousin appeared and Tom yelled to Jack to look for Emily. People screamed and children cried. Most chilling of all, he couldn't hear his son's voice, and in the darkness he hadn't been able to see.

The front of the bus had lurched as it slid onto the frozen pond. At the same time, he'd heard the loud crack of ice breaking. The bus tilted and in seconds the bus slid partially underwater. Water gushed into the bus through gashes ripped in the sides and windows broken during the slide down the mountain. He'd had only minutes to find Ryan and get them both to the surface before the bus slipped deeper into the water.

It probably only took a minute for him to find his son, but it had seemed like forever. Holding Ryan's unconscious body against his chest and with his own lungs about to burst, Tom fought to get out of the wreck and to the surface. When he finally broke through, he swam the short distance to shore, where someone hauled him up onto the ground.

Red-and-blue lights flashed, sirens sounded, people were crying and yelling and screaming. To his relief there were already ambulances, and Tom had fought to get Ryan on one and climbed in with him when Jack appeared with Emily. Tom hauled her into the ambulance. An attendant started to say something to him, looked at Tom and merely nodded. The paramedics hovered over Ryan after a cursory look at Tom and Emily.

She had a head wound with blood streaming over her face and into her hair. Tom collapsed in the ambulance. He had broken bones, sprains, a ruptured spleen, deep cuts and pneumonia. He and Ryan each ended up in surgery. Tom was moved off the critical list after a day, but Ryan lived eleven days on life support.

Tom would never forget the day they'd returned to the ranch and walked into the empty house. Emily had started sobbing. He had embraced her, holding her while she cried quietly, and he'd felt as if his heart was shattering. He couldn't console her. All he could do was tell her he was sorry.

"You couldn't save him. I couldn't save him. We've lost our baby," she cried.

Tom couldn't keep back tears and his throat was raw. He held her close and stroked her head and knew there were no words to console her.

It was a crushing loss they would have to live with all their lives. Her words—"You couldn't save him"—would also be with him the rest of his life.

As he reflected on the difficult times, Tom

wiped his eyes, then ran his hand over the scar on his knee. He would always have scars on his body and his heart from that night. Tom put his head in his hands. He should have been able to save Ryan. It was his fault and he had failed Emily.

He was beginning to get some peace in his life from working on the ranch, beginning to be reconciled to their separation, when Maverick sent the message to Emily.

Now Tom was back with her, and there was no way he could stop their attraction. She was irresistible, yet when they were together, it conjured up all the old hurts.

Tonight was the first time he had kissed Emily since he moved out of the house last year. It had stirred his desire and probably ruined his chances of sleep for the night. How long would they be together? Was she in danger, or was Maverick just a coward who would go away after a while?

Until Tom knew, he wasn't going to leave her alone. He should have saved Ryan. He damn well wasn't going to let Emily get hurt.

He just hoped Nathan caught Maverick soon so life would settle down and he could try to pick up the pieces of his torn-up life again and move on.

He sat for an hour on the porch, gazing into the night, listening for any strange noises. He heard the sound of a frog croaking somewhere nearby. There was a slight breeze. There were no cars on

the residential street. He dozed and woke and finally decided he should be closer to Emily, so he
went inside. Emily had kept some odd pieces of
her uncle's furniture, like the kitchen table and a
rocker, but she'd gotten rid of the beds and sofas,
leaving nowhere to sleep except the floor or his
sleeping bag. Or with Emily.

"Damn," he whispered, thinking he had to get
her out of his thoughts or he would not have another peaceful night until they caught Maverick.
Then he went upstairs quietly and crossed the
room adjoining hers with a door between them left
open. He stretched out on his sleeping bag. He was
asleep instantly. Twice in the night he stirred and
went back to sleep, only to wake before sunrise.

He showered and dressed and went to the kitchen,
where he cooked oatmeal.

As he poured orange juice, he heard footsteps
and then Emily appeared. He was unable to resist
letting his gaze drift to her toes and back up again.
His breath caught in his chest.

"There goes peace and quiet for today," he said.
"What are you trying to do to me, Emily?"

"What? I'm not doing anything except getting
ready to fix breakfast and go to work on this house.
What are you talking about?" she asked.

He walked closer and put his hands on his hips
to look at her. She wore a blue cotton shirt tucked
into cutoffs, ankle socks and tennis shoes. His

gaze roamed over the V-neck of her blouse, down over her tiny waist and her long, long shapely legs. When his gaze slowly drifted up again, she shook her head.

"That's ridiculous. You've seen me like this hundreds of times."

"I'm used to being on the ranch with a bunch of cowhands."

"I think you better work. This place needs a lot done, and you insisted on being here."

"I'll try to concentrate on painting. Right now, I have a pot of oatmeal waiting. There are blueberries, strawberries, orange juice. Let's partake and then I'll work at the opposite end of the house."

She laughed. "You're being ridiculous," she said.

He couldn't smile. By nightfall, she would have him tied in knots. "I hope I can get my hands on this Maverick for just a few minutes," he said quietly. She heard him and smiled, shaking her head because she probably thought he was joking.

As they ate, Tom sipped coffee and looked around. "I sent a text to my friend and he'll be out this morning to look at the house and give you an estimate on the cost of the alarm. I told him it's a rush."

"That's fast, Tom."

"I'm a very good customer. I send a lot of business their way by telling friends and other ranchers about them."

"You're taking charge again."

"I'm just helping you get organized and telling you what I can do to help. I can do other things," he said, unable to resist flirting with her. When she walked into the room, she brought cheer and sunshine that drove away his demons from the night. "We're eating together and we'll work together."

"We'll work together. With you here, I don't know why I need an alarm. Now if you're planning on leaving—" she said cheerfully before he interrupted.

"I'm not leaving you. I'll take you with me if I need to. I'm here until they get Maverick. This place is going to take a whole lot to fix," he said, looking around.

"It's all I have," she answered quietly, looking at the high ceiling in the kitchen. "It's a tie to Mom and Uncle Woody and, really, a tie to when we first got married and after Ryan was born. Uncle Woody was always so happy to see Ryan."

"I remember staying here with you after we married when your uncle went to Chicago to his Shriner convention."

"I remember, too, and all we did was stay in bed. But we're not going to reminisce about that."

"Might be more fun than painting the house," Tom said, and she smiled as she shook her head.

She stood and leaned forward over the table. "You're so good at giving orders. Well, so am I. You clean the kitchen while I get out the paint and brushes."

"Where did Uncle Woody keep his paintbrushes?"

"In the workshop at the back of the garage."

"I think I'll go with you to get them and then I'll clean the kitchen."

"Tom—"

"We've been over this. You don't know how angry Maverick is. Besides, you'll enjoy my company."

"Too bad you don't have more confidence."

He walked around the table as they both carried their dishes to the sink.

"You win," she said with a sigh. "Let's both clean the kitchen and then we'll both go get the paint and brushes."

He worked fast, glancing at her. He had been teasing, but what he'd said to her was the truth. He had been dealing with guys who worked for him, cattle, horses, dusty fields and new calves. To work with her dressed in shorts and a cotton shirt was dazzling, and it was going to be difficult to keep his mind on anything else. Emily was good-looking, and it seemed to him she had gotten more so in the past year. He turned to watch her.

He thought about their kiss yesterday and just as quickly knew that was the way to disaster. He needed to think about getting the house safe. He needed to think about anything except kissing or making love to her. He turned again to look at her, taking his time because her back was still to him. She couldn't reach a shelf to put a bowl away. He crossed the room, took the bowl from her and placed it on the shelf, turning to her.

"Thank you," she said. Her words came out breathless and he knew he should walk away quickly.

He stopped at the door. "Ready to go get paint?"

"Sure. I think we better get to work," she said, heading for the kitchen door. He crossed the room to follow her out. They were kidding and flirting—something that hadn't happened in an incredibly long time, since before he moved out.

Did she want to make love? The thought made the temperature in the room rev up several notches. Did he want the emotional storm again? Looking at her legs and thinking about yesterday's kiss, he realized he did. If he had a chance, he'd take it even if it meant hurting later when they said goodbye. And he knew they would say goodbye no matter what they did during this time while Maverick was on the loose. Their problems were unsolvable and permanent. They had lost their son, and Emily could not get pregnant again and would not adopt because she had wanted a child exactly like Ryan, with their blood in his or her veins. And she blamed him for

Ryan's death. Tom knew he had failed her, failed Ryan, and there was never a day that passed that he didn't think about it.

None of that could stop this lusty desire to seduce her, though.

Tom held the door for her and they walked to the garage, which was dark and stuffy. Tom took one look at the ladder and shook his head. "No way."

"Here we go again. Are you going to tell me I can't use that ladder?"

"I sure as hell am." He stepped on the bottom rung and put all his weight on it. It snapped in two and he dropped to the ground.

"Want to fall today? I'll be glad to catch you. Go ahead and try."

She shook her head. "Okay. You made your point—a new ladder."

He looked around. "Em, you need new paint, new brushes and a new ladder. When was the last time you or your uncle used this stuff?"

"Probably when I was seventeen. I don't remember." She laughed again. "You win that one. Let's go."

He placed his hand on her waist and she stopped instantly, looking up at him. "This reminds me of when we dated. I remember being out here once with you."

She blushed again. "I think we better go."

"Want to know how to make work a little bit fun? Do you remember being here with me?"

"Yes, I remember every single second. You know full well what you can do to me," she answered and this time she was breathless. They might both have regrets, but right now he thought she wanted to kiss as much as he did. Sliding his arm around her waist, he leaned down to kiss her.

The minute his mouth touched hers, he lost the casual, playful attitude he'd had. His tongue went deep as she stood on tiptoe, wound her arms around his neck and pressed against him. She kissed him in return, setting him on fire with longing. He might be sorry tomorrow, but right now, he wanted to kiss her for the rest of the day and the night.

He wound his fingers in her thick, soft hair and ran his other hand down over her enticing bottom. He could easily get his fingers inside her tiny shorts. She gasped and moaned with pleasure, thrusting her hips against him. He wanted her and he was hot, on fire, melting from her kisses and from touching her intimately.

She finally stepped out of his arms and gasped for breath. "We're going to have regrets," she said and turned, walking away swiftly. "You close up," she said over her shoulder and kept going.

He wanted to seduce her. Even knowing that it would cause a world of pain later and complicate his life, that he would have regrets because noth-

ing was going to change between them, he wanted
to make love to her all night long.

He'd known when he told her he was going
to stay with her until they caught Maverick that
he was walking straight into more heartache. He
kicked one of the paint cans and it rolled across
the floor and hit a wall. Why did she have to be
so damned sexy? She'd always appealed to him,
and that had never changed no matter what kind
of heartaches they had between them.

And she wanted to make love. She was at war
with herself and trying to maintain control, but he
could tell what she wanted. When he touched and
kissed her, her response was instant and intense.

He looked at the ladder; it was a piece of junk.
He gathered it up along with the paint cans and
took them out to the big trash barrel. He went back
to close the garage door and fasten the lock. As
he walked back to the house, he wondered if he
could seduce her. He had a sleeping bag and she
had a cot. He didn't care if he had to stand on top
of the car, he wanted her. "Stay away from her," he
said aloud. "Leave her alone. She's trouble. Pure
trouble," he added.

He didn't find her downstairs, but before he
could go up to the second floor to look for her,
she appeared at the top of the stairs. She wore a
long-sleeved T-shirt and jeans and had her hair
in a pigtail.

She came down fast and paused on the bottom step. "Now I should look much more ordinary and unappealing. Less…something."

"Go ahead and say it—less sexy. You'll never look unappealing to me and there will never be a time you are not tempting. But I know we have things to do, so I'll try to avoid looking below your chin or at your cute butt when you walk away. I'll warn you, no matter how you dress, my thoughts are wicked and sinful."

"I believe that one," she said, smiling, and he smiled in return.

"I'm glad we can still get along, Emily."

"Time helps," she said, and she sounded earnest. All the playfulness left her voice. He felt as if there was a very thin veneer of joy and fun and sex appeal, of what they used to have together, and in this rarefied atmosphere, they could enjoy each other's company again. But beyond that, nothing had changed—their close, loving relationship had ended long ago.

Tom's friend came from the alarm company and Tom joined her while they settled on the alarm system with the stipulation that it would be installed Monday…

At noon, they decided to take a break from their errands and went to the Royal Diner again for another burger.

"Yesterday when we left here, I didn't think I

would ever be here again to eat a burger with you. Here I am less than twenty-four hours later. I didn't think that would be possible," Emily said.

"Just goes to show, expect more and maybe you'll get more."

"Right."

After a few minutes, he smiled at her. "I'm glad your photography is going well."

"I like it and I'm getting customers from other towns. I may just move to Dallas if business continues to grow. I'll keep Uncle Woody's house—"

"Em, it's your house now. You can stop calling it Uncle Woody's," Tom said, but his thoughts were on her moving to Dallas. When she said that, he felt another stab of loss. Instantly, he knew that was ridiculous because when their divorce went through, he and Emily would go their separate ways. He tried to avoid thinking about the future and pay attention to what she was saying to him.

"It's difficult to remember that this is my house now. Frankly, it's still Uncle Woody's to me even though I own it." She sipped her malt and after a few minutes asked, "Do you miss the military?"

Tom shook his head. "No. I've served and I'm glad to be on the ranch now. Life hasn't turned out the way I expected it to, but I love the ranch. Frankly, Em, losing Jeremy took it out of me. That one hurt more than the others. Maybe it's because of losing Ryan and because I'm older now, but I've had enough of death and my buddies getting hurt."

"You were patriotic serving your country," she said, placing her hand on his. Instantly, he inhaled. She blinked and started to jerk her hand away, but he covered it and held it between his.

"That's nice. Don't pull away," he said softly.

"We're both doing things that will make it worse. We'll be hurt all over again because our future hasn't changed and isn't going to."

He felt a pinch to his heart and released her hand. "You're right," he said. "If I pass the sheriff's office and Nathan is there, I'll see what I can find out. I'm sure nothing eventful has happened or we would have heard something."

"We'll have the meeting at the TCC Monday morning."

"I hope this balmy spring weather holds, because we can keep the house aired out as we paint." He nodded and they lapsed into silence as they finished their burgers and then left to get her painting supplies.

When they returned to the house, she propped the front door open. "Tom, the paint fumes will be awful. There's an attic fan that will draw fresh air through and take out the fumes. I want to open the windows that are left and turn it on."

"That's fine with me. Another thing—I'll do

the ceilings. Let me do the high stuff and you stay off the ladder."

"There's no end to your orders. You're no longer in the military, remember?"

"And you never were in it and you don't take orders worth a damn," he said, smiling and shaking his head.

"That definitely isn't so. Here you are, staying with me. I didn't think that one up. I'm not getting on the ladder. I didn't make that decision. I'm getting an alarm because of you. I've moved upstairs because of you."

"You won't let me kiss you. I have to catch you by surprise and then you run me off," he said, moving closer and looking into her big green eyes.

"Not so," she said, smiling. "You kiss me every time you decide you want to and you know it," she said, poking his hard stomach with her forefinger as if to emphasize what she was saying. "Mmm, that's impressive," she said, poking him again.

"Let's see if you'll let me kiss you just any old time," he said, wrapping his arms around her and leaning over her. His mouth covered and opened hers, his tongue going deep as he leaned farther until she clung to him and kissed him in return and he forgot their silly conversation. Holding her tightly, he straightened up and his arm tightened around her waist while he slowly ran his hand down her back and over her bottom. Then his hand drifted up and he unbuttoned her blouse as he kissed her. He caressed her breast, pushing away her bra.

She finally caught his hand and held it. "Tom, wait. Don't complicate our lives. You know where we're headed—for more hurt," she whispered, looking up at him. He gazed at her intently. He was aroused, hard and ready. He wanted her and he didn't think she would argue. As he gazed at her, he thought about the rift between them and knew she really didn't want his loving.

"You're right. We've hurt each other enough," he said softly. "I'll get the windows open and start painting downstairs."

Five

Tom stood on the new ladder, painting the front parlor ceiling, while Emily painted upstairs in one of the big bedrooms. He'd been at it for hours. At a certain point, he had changed to cutoffs and a sleeveless T-shirt because the air-conditioning was off since the house was open.

As Tom worked he thought about her living in the big house all alone. She might be thinking the same thing about him on the ranch, but he never felt alone there. He worked with guys all day and he could go find someone whenever he wanted to. And when they divorced he would be able to get a date when he wanted. But at this point in his life, he couldn't imagine wanting to go out with someone. The thought of Emily doing so was another deep hurt.

His estrangement from Emily had left Tom numb and hurting, and his life would have to change a lot before he would ever want to get involved with someone again. He was surprised how well he was getting along with Emily, because it really hurt to be together and he knew it hurt her. Their divorce had merely been tabled until later but definitely loomed in the near future.

He thought about the big, expensive mansion they had built on the ranch. He didn't want to go back to it, yet it was a tie to Ryan—it was where they'd brought him home from the hospital. Where they'd rocked him to sleep and read to him, sung him songs.

What could Tom do with the house? He had no idea, and he didn't intend to worry about it now.

He wiped his sweaty forehead and tried to concentrate on his brushstrokes and keep working steadily. When he finished this side of the room, he was taking a break and going to find Emily.

After another hour of work, Tom ordered pizzas for dinner. When they were done with their break they returned to painting.

It was after 11:00 p.m. when he went to find her again in the front parlor. She was on her knees, painting the baseboard, and his gaze roamed over her trim, very sexy ass. He inhaled deeply and knocked on the open door.

Emily looked up and sat back on her haunches as Tom entered. "You're just in time. I'm getting tired of this and I think the paint fumes are getting to me even with the windows open and the fans blowing."

"Let's knock off for tonight, sit on the porch and have a cold drink, and just relax. It's do-nothing time." He crossed the room to her and took her brush. "I'll clean the brushes."

"And I'll get the drinks," she said, standing and looking at the painting she had done. Tom put the lid on her paint can and then picked up the other brushes.

"Let's get out of here. We need fresh air and I want a cold beer."

"I want a drink, too. See you on the porch."

She got there first and sat in one of the big wooden rocking chairs. She had brought beer for Tom and iced tea for herself. It was cool on the porch, and in minutes her eyes adjusted to the darkness. Tom came out and picked up a small table with their drinks to place it slightly in front of their chairs and then moved his rocking chair closer to hers.

"Now the view is better here," he said when he sat down.

"Liar. You can't enjoy the view in all this darkness. You just wanted to sit closer together," she said, amused by him. "It's nice out here."

"Yes, it is, and it's nicer closer together."

"It's wonderful you've been helping the Valentines. You're a good guy and I still feel so foolish for believing that email. That was a huge mistake."

"Forget that, Em. We worked it out, and Natalie invited us to a picnic in the park next Saturday, if you want. I told her I'd call her after I talk to you."

"Saturday's fine."

"Can you skip painting long enough for a picnic?"

"Of course. I have your help with painting and I hadn't planned on that. I'd like to meet them. Once again, I hope whoever Maverick is, word gets back that we're all having a good time together."

"The way word gets around Royal, I suspect it will. You'll like Natalie. After her loss, she understands ours in a way some people really don't. Jeremy was a great guy. We were close—he was almost like a brother to me. Sometimes the stuff you go through when your life is at stake creates a real bond."

"I should have known you wouldn't have a secret family."

"As you said, the picture was convincing."

They sat quietly in the dark while she sipped her raspberry tea and Tom drank his beer. She watched the shifting shadows on the lawn. "I still think you should go back to the ranch. I can get this done."

"Nope. I'm staying, and you should let me do the high stuff in every room."

"Oh, my. If you're volunteering to paint the ceilings in this old house, I will take you up on that with joy. I figured I would hire a painter to do the ceilings, but if you're sure, that fun task is yours. I'm thrilled because I can't do them."

"I'll start on the ceilings and see how far I can get. When and if they catch Maverick, I'm gone. You know that."

"Of course. I know you didn't move in permanently."

"Somehow I can't imagine you here permanently."

"I don't know why—I lived here when we met. We were together in this house lots of times."

"I was just noticing how dark it is out here. The branches of these big oaks almost touch the ground, and they give a lot of privacy. When I move out, I think you should have yard lights and motion detectors installed."

"By the time you get through, I'll have a chain-link fence with razor wire at the top and spotlights. You were in the Rangers too long and in scary, violent situations too much. This is Royal, Tom. All the precautions aren't necessary. We're safe here. And no one cares what we're doing behind the branches of the oak tree."

"You think?" he asked, setting down his bottle of beer. "Well, if we have privacy and no one cares what we do, I think I'm wasting a really good night by sitting over here alone." He stood and she wondered what he was up to now.

He leaned over to pick her up and then sat down again with her on his lap. She gasped in surprise and started to protest, but she liked being in his arms again, so she closed her mouth and wrapped her arm around his neck instead. "It's as dark as a cave out here tonight. I can't see you," she said quietly. "What brought this on?"

"Why not? We've got privacy to do what we want—you just said so. Why not forget our problems for ten minutes and enjoy each other's company and a few kisses besides? Or more."

She smiled as she ran her fingers through his hair. "You really have a one-track mind."

"No, I've been alone for a long time," he replied. "And now I'm with you. That's the biggest part of it."

His voice was low, the way it got when he was lusty. She was aware of being in his arms, on his lap. Even more, she was aware of his arousal. He flirted and teased the way he used to, so it was fun to be with him.

"You're not only a good guy. You're a very sexy guy."

"Is that right? On a scale of one to ten, where do I rate?" he asked, nuzzling her neck.

"Somewhere around one hundred," she said, her words coming out breathlessly and as if she barely thought about what she said. "But I'm not going to let you complicate my life tonight. I've spent the past year picking up the pieces and I'm on a shaky foundation—"

"This will get you on something solid."

"You're naughty, Tom," she replied as he trailed kisses across her neck and ran his tongue around the curve of her ear.

"But, oh, so sexy. You just said so." He kissed away her answer. His mouth covered hers, his arm tightening around her as he leaned her against his shoulder. She clung to him, kissing him in return. His kisses sizzled, making her want more loving from him.

He raised his head and yanked off his shirt, tossing it aside while she said, "For just a minute more, Tom. That's all we—"

He leaned close to kiss her again and end her talk. And she didn't care. She clung to him, thinking he was the most exciting man on earth and trying to avoid thinking about all the painful things that had come between them.

He caressed her breast and then slipped his hand

beneath her shirt. His hand was warm, his palm rough and callused. He unfastened her bra easily and pushed it away. She moaned with pleasure as her breast filled his hand. His thumb circled the taut peak and she shifted her hips closer against him—as close as possible while she arched her back and gave him more access to caress her further. For the moment she was lost to the sensations he stirred up. His hands on her, his mouth on her—it seemed natural and right and made her want more. But the memories of past heartache were still strong. Suddenly she thought back to the last time they'd made love—he'd moved out immediately after.

"Tom, wait." She paused to look at him as she placed her hand on his jaw and felt the short stubble beneath her fingers and palm. "You're going to bring back all that we're trying to get away from."

"Live a little, darlin'. We should just let go and enjoy each other and the night. You can't tell me you don't like this."

"You know I love everything you do," she said, "but we've tried every way possible to work things out and haven't even come close." She wiggled away and slipped off his lap. "It's time for me to go upstairs."

He didn't answer. She left her drink and turned to hurry inside. She wanted to be in his arms, ached to have him carry her to bed and make love to her all night long. But if he did, morning would come and with it painful choices. They would go back to the way they were and it would hurt more than ever. She couldn't stay on that seesaw of hot sex and then estrangement. He couldn't have it both ways. Besides, she knew the night he moved out to the guesthouse, he had meant it to be for good.

She rushed upstairs, fighting with herself silently every second because she really wanted to go right back to him. But it would be futile and lead to more hurt. She grabbed clothes and went to her shower, hoping he didn't come upstairs until she was asleep.

Finally she was settled beneath the sheets on her cot. The house was still open, the windows flung wide, but Tom would take care of everything downstairs and lock up. She didn't have to worry about any of it. What she had to worry about was Tom causing her to fall in love with him again.

She rolled over on her back and stared at the open windows. Her thoughts were on tonight and Tom. She couldn't fall in love with him again. She wasn't going through what they had before. She couldn't get pregnant and give him another son. Or a daughter. It wasn't going to happen. It had hurt to tell him over and over that she was not pregnant.

It was more than an hour later when she heard a board creak and then all was quiet. She closed her eyes and lay still, wondering if he would come see if she was asleep. She couldn't deal with him again tonight. She was torn between wanting to pull him down on the cot with her and avoiding any physical contact. His lovemaking could take her out of the world, but then later, regret would consume her.

The next morning she showered and dressed, pulling on a sleeveless pale blue cotton dress to wear to church. She brushed her wavy hair that fell loosely around her face. Stepping into blue high heels, she picked up her envelope purse, took a deep breath and went downstairs to breakfast.

When she entered the kitchen, Tom came to his feet and her heart lurched as her gaze ran over his white shirt, red tie and navy suit. "You look handsome enough to have breakfast with," she said. "Oh, my."

"You look gorgeous, Em," he said in a husky voice. "I fixed cheese grits with shrimp. Your orange juice is poured."

"Thank you," she said. She had already left her purse on a folding chair in the front room. She crossed the room to pour coffee. "Let me guess—you're going to church with me because of Maverick."

"That and because you're the best-looking, sexiest woman in the county."

She laughed and turned toward him. He took the coffee from her hand and set it on the counter, and her pulse raced. His arm circled her waist and she placed her hand lightly against his chest. "You'll wrinkle me," she said, trying to ignore the heat building inside her.

He dropped his hand, leaned forward and placed his mouth on hers without touching her anywhere else. She was as lost in his kiss as she would have been if he had embraced her. Desire rocked her, and she wrapped her arms around him, stepping close to hold him tightly while she kissed him in return and forgot about wrinkles and her dress.

He made a sound deep in his throat and his arms wrapped around her tightly, holding her against him. His kiss was demanding, making her want to kiss him back and shower kisses on him the rest of the day.

Instead, she stepped away and gulped for breath. "Do you do that just to see if you still can? If that's why, I'll tell you that yes, you can turn me to mush and set me on fire at the same time." She stared at him a moment and then walked away quickly. "I'm going to church."

"Come eat your breakfast. You have time and I'll get out of here," he said and left the room.

She closed her eyes momentarily, trying to get composed. Her lips tingled and she wanted to make love. She ate a few bites of the cheese grits, drank some orange juice and coffee and left it all until later to clean. She hurried upstairs and brushed her teeth. When she came back downstairs and grabbed her purse, Tom was nowhere around. She had already decided it would be a good day for her to walk.

She opened the door to leave, and as she crossed the porch, he stepped up to walk beside her. "I'll drive you there."

"I was going to walk."

"Let's take the car. You'll be a few minutes early. When you walk, you may be as safe as money in the bank vault, but humor me. I don't like you getting a message from Maverick and I can't relax about it."

"I understand," she said, trying to be patient but thinking he was being overly protective.

"You win the prize for the correct answer."

"I'm trying, too, Tom. I know your background makes you think the way you do and I know this will end. Maverick will be caught or stop sending messages and disappear. Before long we'll go our separate ways," she said, feeling a tightness in her chest when she said those last words.

"We'll get the divorce as soon as this is over," he said, sounding tense. "I've been thinking about that. We can work it out ourselves, turn it over to our attorneys."

"I think we can work this out. I know you'll

be not only fair but generous, because that's the way you are."

"Thanks," he said in a flat voice that indicated this was hard for him. He held open her car door, closing it after she was seated.

As he drove away from the house, he glanced at her. "I've thought about our divorce. We can get a dollar figure on what the ranch and livestock are worth and I can buy you out. We can add the vehicles and the plane to that estimate and I'll pay you for those. You keep your car. We won't count it."

His hands gripped the steering wheel tightly. She knew him well, and knew by his tone of voice that he was unhappy.

"We don't have to decide yet," she said.

"We might as well make the decisions and be ready. When the time comes, it'll be easier and quicker and then we can say goodbye." He drew a deep breath and she hurt inside.

When he parked at the church, he walked around the car to open the door for her.

"Thank you," she said as she emerged into sunshine.

"Smile. We don't know this troll's identity, but I want Maverick to see that his damned email didn't do anything except get us together." She smiled and he took her arm. She thought they probably looked like a happy couple. She hoped the person hiding behind the name Maverick thought they were happily together again. Then she recalled how shocked she had been looking at the picture of Tom and the Valentines. Next Saturday she would meet them, and she was looking forward to it. She glanced up at Tom, sorry she had doubted him. He was a wonderful guy who had been a good dad and husband. That's what hurt so badly.

After church he took her to eat at the Texas Cattleman's Club, and afterward they drove back to her house to paint again. It was the first Sunday in March and it was a perfect spring day. She pulled on cutoffs and another T-shirt.

She found him downstairs in the front parlor, prying open a can of white paint. Plastic drop cloths covered the hardwood floor. The ladder stood to one side and he had papers spread with brushes and stir sticks laid out.

"Calm yourself, because you've seen me in shorts and less plenty of times," she said when she joined him to get the can of paint he had opened for her.

He straightened, turning to look at her.

"Although I think I'm the one who might not be able to concentrate," she amended, fanning herself as her gaze roamed over him. Tom was all muscle, in excellent physical shape and incredibly strong. She tried to avoid memories of making love and how exciting he could be. As her gaze drifted over him again, she looked up and met his hazel eyes.

"We could put off painting," he said in a husky voice.

She shook her head even though she didn't want to. "Did you open a can of paint for me?" Her voice was raspy and she couldn't stop looking at his broad shoulders.

He stepped over the paint cans and approached her. She threw up both hands. "I'm going to work. Give me the paint. I have to get this house painted, and you're here now and can help."

"What room? I'll carry it for you," he said.

"The front bedroom," she said, turning to go. He walked beside her. "We've already lost the morning and part of the afternoon. I want to get something done today." She felt as if she was babbling. In the bedroom she waved her hand. "Thanks. I'll start here and work my way around."

He put the can on the floor, turned to her, stepped close and caught her chin lightly in his fingers. "You want to kiss and so do I."

"I'm trying to be sensible and not complicate our lives more. Not to mention getting my house painted."

"See which you like best," he said and drew her close, leaning down to kiss her. She stood in his arms for about two seconds before she hugged him back, sliding her hand over his broad shoulders and down one arm over rock-hard biceps. Then she wrapped her arms around his narrow waist. It always amazed her how narrow his waist was and how flat his stomach. She finally stopped him and stepped back, trying to catch her breath, pulling her T-shirt down.

"We could make love and get that out of our systems."

She smiled at him. "Good try."

He grinned and shrugged. "It's definitely worth a try. I might bring that up again after you've painted for seven or eight hours and the sun goes down."

"You can try me and see," she said in a sultry voice, unable to resist flirting with him.

Something flickered in the depths of his eyes, and a faint smile raised the corner of his mouth. "Ah, I think I'm on the right track. I will try again. That's a promise." He stepped close and touched the corner of her mouth. "It's good to see you smile and laugh. We used to have lots of smiles and laughs and it's nice to share them again."

"It's temporary, Tom. Nothing has changed," she stated, hurting because of all they had lost and still stood to lose.

His smile faded. "I know."

"Now, it's time for you to go to work, too, and make yourself useful. You insisted on this," she said, picking up a brush.

He leaned close and placed his hand on her shoulders. She looked into his eyes and was aware his mouth was only inches away. She drew a deep breath, wanting to kiss him and knowing she should not.

"I can make myself not only useful, but indispensable," he said as he ran his hands so lightly along her bare thighs, then sliding them to the insides of her legs.

She placed a paintbrush in his hand. "You go paint and stop with the seduction scene."

"I thought I was doing pretty good."

She leaned forward so her nose almost touched his. "You know you're doing damn good, so you have to go or this house will never get painted," she said.

"Suit yourself, darlin'. I'm ready, willing and able."

"Ready, willing and able to pick up a brush and paint? Great. Go do it and I will, too. Goodbye, Tom." She turned away and bent over to pick up the paint can and received a whistle of appreciation from him. She straightened up and spun around, but he was already going out the door. Smiling, she shook her head. It was all a lot of foolishness, but if she had taken him up on any of his offers they would be making love now, and that made her hot and tingly and wanting him back holding her close.

She dreaded going through the divorce. It would be another wrenching, painful loss, but it was inevitable. They had tried to stay married, but it didn't work and just hurt more as time passed.

She got busy painting, a routine chore that left her thoughts free. And Tom filled them. Before Maverick's email, she'd thought she was beginning to achieve some peace. She'd been adjusting to life without Tom, as well as the realization that he would be out of her life for good when they divorced. Life on the ranch, which she had loved in so many ways, would also be gone. But she was beginning to find a life for herself as a photographer. She had made the move from the ranch to Royal. Now she had been thrown a curveball when Tom came to stay with her. They were flirting, laughing together—something that didn't happen after they lost Ryan. A week ago she wouldn't have guessed that they could be this relaxed together again. Maybe it was because they had lost everything they'd once had between them. Now the worst had happened and she didn't feel as tense. Maybe she had worried too much about disappointing Tom, and the fear was a self-fulfilling prophecy. It was fun to tease and flirt again. She missed what she'd once had with Tom.

Whatever the reasons, working with him on the house now reminded her of old times together when they could flirt and kiss and laugh. It was also going to hurt a lot more to tell him goodbye after being here together.

It was almost midnight when they settled in the rocking chairs on the porch. Tom had his cold beer and she had her raspberry tea and they sat quietly rocking.

"I remember when Uncle Woody would come out here and mow the lawn. He'd wave to anyone who passed and talk to neighbors who walked by."

"Your uncle was a friendly man. I liked him. When you and I dated, sometimes he gave me a look and I wondered if he was going to tell me to get lost and leave you alone."

"No. Uncle Woody liked you and thought you were good for me."

"That's nice to hear."

"I'm glad he didn't know about our divorce. I think losing Ryan is what—" She paused, because she hadn't ever voiced aloud her theory about her uncle's death. Tears threatened and she was grateful for the dark.

"Was what?" Tom asked and his voice had changed, deepened and become serious.

"I think he just died of a broken heart. He wasn't well, but he wasn't that ill. He had a heart problem, but when Ryan died, part of Uncle Woody died and there was never a time I saw him after that when he didn't cry over Ryan. It broke his heart. So I lost them both."

Tom sat in silence and she wondered what was

going through his mind. She wiped her eyes, gradually regaining her composure.

"I'm going for a walk around the place. I have my phone if you want me," he said tersely. Then he faded into the darkness.

Tom walked around the property, staying in shadows, moving without making noise and taking his time.

Emily's revelation about her uncle's death hurt. Tom had no doubt that Woody had blamed him for his failure to save Ryan. He felt equally certain Woody had blamed Tom for Emily's unhappiness. He was just one more person who was important to Tom that he had failed.

He finally decided to rejoin Emily on the porch or just sit there alone if she had gone inside. But when he got back to the front of the house, she was still there. He climbed the steps to sit by her.

"You're back. This is nice, Tom. I'll miss us out here together when you go," she said quietly.

"Maybe I'll come visit and we can sit and talk. I like this, too. This is peaceful, and I can always hope I might get a kiss or two or get you to sit on my lap."

"No," she said, a note of sadness in her voice. "After our divorce, you'll go out, fall in love and marry again. You'll have a family, because that is what you were meant for. You're wonderful with kids. You and I will go our separate ways and our marriage will just be memories that fade into oblivion." She stood. "I'm going inside."

He came to his feet swiftly and wrapped his arms around her to kiss her, a hard, possessive kiss that took only seconds before she responded.

When he slipped his hand beneath her shirt and caressed her, she moaned softly, holding him until she suddenly stepped away.

"I can't go there. We'll just hurt each other more. I've disappointed you in the past and I don't see any future. Making love just binds us together for more heartache. I'm going in." She swept past him and he let her go.

She didn't want him in her life. He had failed her, disappointed her, hurt her. He needed to let her go and keep his distance and hope they caught Maverick soon. He couldn't live under the same roof with her much longer without making love, and he had no doubt that he could get her to agree, but afterward, their relationship might be worse than ever because that wasn't what Emily wanted. She wanted him out of her life. She was moving to Royal, taking up photography, finding a new life for herself, and he should do the same. He should find happiness with someone he hadn't failed and hurt and disappointed.

He stepped off the porch to circle around the big yard, wishing he could catch the troll and end his worries about Emily once and for all.

Six

Monday morning they drove the short distance to the Texas Cattleman's Club for the emergency meeting about Maverick.

Tom parked and they walked together toward the front door. Emily looked at the dark stone-and-wood clubhouse. In recent years, the TCC had voted to include women. It still hurt to walk in the front door and see the children's center where she had taken Ryan occasionally.

She waited while Tom checked his black Stetson. He wore a tan sport coat, a white dress shirt open at the throat and dark jeans, and just looking at him, her heart beat faster.

He turned and his gaze swept over her, and for another moment, she forgot everyone around them and saw only Tom. She took a deep breath. She would soon be divorced from him. Their marriage was over. Life was changing, and it was difficult to worry about Maverick when she had lost Ryan and now was losing Tom. Their happy marriage had been gone a long time, though, even if the past few days with him had reminded her of how it used to be.

Looking back now, she realized she had made a big mistake with Tom in being so desperate to get pregnant. That had made her tense and nervous on top of the grief they both dealt with daily.

Now she realized she had driven Tom away. For the past few days, she hadn't had her old worries about her inability to get pregnant, and she was relaxed with him.

At the time she hadn't realized what a mistake she'd made with him, and now it was too late to undo it.

"You look pretty," he said when he walked up to her. He leaned close to speak in her ear. "When you get home, take your hair down."

She smiled at him as she reached up, unfastened the clip that held her hair and shook her head. Her wavy, honey-brown hair fell around her face and on her shoulders.

"I like that," he said softly. He took her arm.

"Let's get a seat." He turned and she walked beside him. They went through the foyer lined with oil paintings of past members. The motto of the club from its early days—Loyalty, Justice and Peace— was emblazoned on the wall in big letters for all to see.

They went past a lounge, and Emily saw a boar's head hanging above a credenza that held a crystal decanter on a silver tray. Some members wanted the stuffed animal heads removed. But they'd had been fascinating to Ryan, and as far as Emily was concerned, they could stay because other little kids might find them just as interesting.

She and Tom greeted friends as they walked through the club. Taking in her surroundings, she couldn't believe the club was more than a hundred years old. It had been founded around 1910 by Henry "Tex" Langley and other local ranchers. Tex wouldn't recognize a lot of things about the club now, particularly that women had been accepted as members, which had resulted in a child-care center where the billiard room once was.

They finally arrived at the large meeting room and settled in near the back. She had an eerie feeling when she thought about how Tom had said Maverick might be present at the meeting. As the room began to fill, she wasn't surprised to see the mean girl trio, Cecelia, Simone and Naomi, arrive and take seats near the front. Could the three

YOUR PARTICIPATION IS REQUESTED!

Dear Reader,

Since you are a lover of our books – we would like to get to know you!

Inside you will find a short Reader's Survey. Sharing your answers with us will help our editorial staff understand who you are and what activities you enjoy.

To thank you for your participation, we would like to send you 2 books and 2 gifts – **ABSOLUTELY FREE!**

Enjoy your gifts with our appreciation,

Pam Powers

SEE INSIDE FOR READER'S SURVEY

For Your Reading Pleasure...

We'll send you 2 books and 2 gifts
ABSOLUTELY FREE
just for completing our Reader's Survey!

YOUR READER'S SURVEY
"THANK YOU" FREE GIFTS INCLUDE:
▶ **2 FREE books**
▶ **2 lovely surprise gifts**

▶ DETACH AND MAIL CARD TODAY! ▶

PLEASE FILL IN THE CIRCLES COMPLETELY TO RESPOND

1) What type of fiction books do you enjoy reading? (Check all that apply)
- ○ Suspense/Thrillers
- ○ Action/Adventure
- ○ Modern-day Romances
- ○ Historical Romance
- ○ Humor
- ○ Paranormal Romance

2) What attracted you most to the last fiction book you purchased on impulse?
- ○ The Title
- ○ The Cover
- ○ The Author
- ○ The Story

3) What is usually the greatest influencer when you <u>plan</u> to buy a book?
- ○ Advertising
- ○ Referral
- ○ Book Review

4) How often do you access the internet?
- ○ Daily
- ○ Weekly
- ○ Monthly
- ○ Rarely or never

5) How many NEW paperback fiction novels have you purchased in the past 3 months?
- ○ 0 - 2
- ○ 3 - 6
- ○ 7 or more

YES! I have completed the Reader's Survey. Please send me the 2 FREE books and 2 FREE gifts (gifts are worth about $10 retail) for which I qualify. I understand that I am under no obligation to purchase any books, as explained on the back of this card.

225/326 HDL GLNZ

FIRST NAME	LAST NAME

ADDRESS

APT.#	CITY

STATE/PROV.	ZIP/POSTAL CODE

© 2016 ENTERPRISES LIMITED
® and ™ are trademarks owned and used by the trademark owner and/or its licensee. Printed in the U.S.A.

women be behind the emails and blackmail? That was the rumor. But Emily couldn't imagine them doing something that wicked and then coming to this meeting. They were members of the TCC and had had background checks, friends in the club and people to vouch for them. They might be snooty, but she didn't think any one of them would do something criminal. She'd heard that Maverick blackmailed Brandee Lawless. And why would they have come after her, sending her that photo of Tom with the Valentines? How would they have even gotten such a photo?

"There's Nathan," Tom said and she glanced around the room. Sheriff Battle stood to one side, leaning against the wall, looking as if he wasn't paying attention, but she knew he probably wasn't missing anything that was happening in the big room.

At the stroke of the hour, Case appeared. Whenever she saw him, he looked in a hurry. Often he talked fast. His brown suit matched his short dark brown hair, and he looked as if he hadn't shaved for a couple of days.

"Good morning and thanks for coming," he said, holding a mike and stepping out from behind a podium they had set up for him.

People in the audience answered with an enthusiastic, "Good morning."

"Everyone here knows why we're having this

meeting. We have a problem in Royal. Someone going by the name of Maverick is harassing and blackmailing people using social media and email. We need to put a stop to it." Case paused to allow for applause.

"I'd like to form a TCC committee to investigate, coordinating with the sheriff to back up his department's work. We're not law enforcement— just a group of concerned club members, citizens of Royal, who will make a big effort to keep their eyes and ears open for anything that might aid Sheriff Battle. You can sign up at the door and you'll be notified when we'll have our first meeting.

"Also, Chelsea Hunt has asked if she may speak. She has some ideas of her own that should help. Chelsea, why don't you come up here?"

Wearing head-turning designer jeans with a tucked-in white silk shirt and a leather vest, Chelsea walked up to join Case, amid more applause. Her high-heeled ankle boots made Chelsea appear to be the same height as the club president.

"Here comes the tech genius. She'll get things moving," Tom said quietly as he applauded. Emily knew that Chelsea was considered the cyber expert in Royal, so she was a good one to have at the meeting.

"I'm glad all of you are here today. I'm fully committed to the TCC's grassroots investigation into these cyber attacks. I'll have a tablet here at the front, so when the meeting is over, if you have computer skills and want to help me with the technical aspects of the investigation, please sign up. There has to be a way to find Maverick. There will be a trail of some sort, and I think if we pool resources, we can trace these messages."

Everyone applauded again and Chelsea thanked Case and sat down.

Tom stood and Case turned to him. "Tom?"

"I think we need to get word out to citizens in Royal. If they get a message from Maverick, they need to let Sheriff Battle know, even if there's blackmail involved. We can't do anything if we don't know who Maverick is targeting."

"I think we can all work on getting that message out," Case said, nodding. "Thanks." Tom sat back down.

Emily wondered how many people already knew she had received an email. She knew Tom and Nathan would only tell people on a need-to-know basis, so she suspected that not many were aware of her situation.

"Simone," Case said, recognizing Simone Parker, one of the mean girls triumvirate. There was instant quiet. Simone's striking looks, her blue eyes and long black hair usually commanded everyone's attention.

"I think we should have another meeting here

in a month so the committee can bring the rest of us up-to-date on what's been done. The more informed TCC members are, the better we can deal with what's happening."

"We can do that," Case said. "If there are things Sheriff Battle thinks should not be made public, then they won't be, but otherwise, we'll meet again next month. Unless Maverick is caught in the meantime."

As Emily listened to the other speakers' suggestions, she looked over the club members in attendance. Once again she couldn't help wondering if the troll was in the audience.

How would they ever catch Maverick? What had she done to make herself a target of this troll? She still couldn't imagine someone being so angry with her that they would send that nasty message with the picture.

Finally, the meeting was over and Tom left her side to sign up for the committee. When he was done, he found Emily and took her arm to lead her out. His touch was as electrifying as ever. Why did he have that effect on her after all they had been through?

"I hope that meeting helped," she said as they drove back to her house. "Tom, shouldn't you go back to the ranch and check on things?"

"I will later this week. I talk to Gus several times a day and I'm available. This isn't the first time I've been away from there, and it hasn't been long yet. We're just getting started on this. It may take a long time to catch this Maverick character, but I have high hopes in Chelsea. If I were the troll and had Chelsea after me, I would be worried. Nathan, too. Nathan is quiet and easygoing, but he's tough and he doesn't miss a thing."

"I hope they can discover something soon," she said, wondering if living with Tom much longer would make it even more difficult to part again.

"I hope so, too," he said, but he didn't sound too happy about it.

"Stop at the grocery and let's pick up what we need to make sandwiches for lunch. It's a pretty day and we can eat on the porch. I don't even have a table."

"Take some furniture from the house at the ranch. The guys will move it for you. Just tell me or Gus what you want."

"Thank you. There are a few things I'd like, but in general, I don't want to move much from the ranch. Your cook likes Snowball so much, I may leave him with her because he likes the ranch."

"That's fine with me."

They bought groceries and when they were back in the car, he turned to her. "Why don't you buy a bed while I'm with you—"

She started laughing. "You've always been a little more subtle in your approach than this. Getting tired of your sleeping bag, or do you think you're going to coax me into bed?"

He raised his eyebrows. "Now that's a thought. I might give that one a try. Seriously, I suggested a bed because I can help you get it moved where you want it. You can get one delivered and set up, but they aren't going to move it around while you make up your mind where you would like it. As I recall on the last bed, I moved it until I wanted to put wheels on it."

"It wasn't that bad," she said, knowing he was teasing her. "When I get a bed, I'll probably go to Dallas or Midland. Though Royal has a good furniture store, so I suppose we can look here."

"Good. Let's look on the way back to the house. You can wait a few more minutes for lunch, I'm sure."

"Okay. We'll get a bed, Tom, but I still think you have at least one other motive besides helping me move it around," she said, watching him drive and wishing they could be like this all the time.

He smiled. "I might. We'll see if you object."

"You usually get what you want," she said, wanting to reach over and touch him just to have a physical connection. At one time she wouldn't have hesitated, but again, those times were over.

"That's interesting. Why do you think I get my way?"

"It's your good looks, your charm, your incredibly sexy body and your seductive ways, of course," she said in a sultry voice, teasing him.

"I may wreck the car. Now I know you need to hurry up and buy that bed."

"Don't rush me."

"I wouldn't think of rushing you to bed. This is something that will take some testing and touching to see if it feels right," he drawled in an exaggeratedly husky voice.

"Stop it," she said, smiling. "I never, ever guessed you and I would go shopping for a bed again."

"Life's full of surprises, and this is a damn fine one."

"I agree," she said, turning toward him as much as her seat belt would allow. "This is like our lives used to be."

"I told you before and I'll tell you again—we can still enjoy each other even though there are some terrible times behind us and some rough times up ahead."

"I've made big mistakes, and I can't undo them. But I'm glad you forgave me for the mistake I made believing Maverick's message. I'm thankful for that."

"We've both made mistakes," he said, suddenly serious, and she wondered what he felt he had done wrong. "Here we are," he said, stopping to park in the shade in front of the furniture store. He stepped out of the car and the moment for discussing their past was gone.

They shopped for almost an hour before she finally pointed to a fruitwood four-poster with a high, intricately carved headboard.

"I like this four-poster. And I like that sleigh bed. What do you think?" she asked, too aware that his opinion didn't matter because she would not be sharing the bed with him.

"I think the four-poster is great. Sleigh beds—even king-size sleigh beds—are too short. There is a tiny off chance I might get into this bed sometime."

"Shall we take bets on how many hours after purchase?" she asked sweetly and he grinned. "A sleigh bed is never too short for me," she said, studying the two frames. "Okay, I guess I'll get the four-poster."

"That's an excellent choice. Let's find the mattresses."

"You're very anxious to get a bed in my house," she said.

"I want you to be comfortable. You never know when you'll really want a bed. I'm sure you're enjoying your cot as much as I'm enjoying my sleeping bag," he said and then frowned slightly. "What's wrong, Em?"

"I started to say I should get a bed for the guest room now, too, but I don't have family. Uncle

Woody was the last except the cousins, and I never see them. My family is gone. You and I will get our divorce and you'll be gone. I don't need a guest bed."

He put his arm around her shoulders. "You'll have a family soon enough. I know you'll marry again. You can wait and get another bed for the guest room some other day, but you need one for yourself now."

She felt the tears threatening. "What happened to us, Tom?"

He pulled her around to hug her. There was no one in that corner of the store and he really didn't care if there was. "We had the most devastating loss, and we just made too many mistakes dealing with that. But maybe some of them can be fixed," he said, holding her close.

She pulled away and wiped her eyes. "We're in public. I'll pull myself together. It's just a little scary to know I'm alone."

"You're not alone. Look, you can call me anytime you want."

She smiled at him. "Sure, Tom. I'm sure your next wife will just be thrilled to hear that you told your ex to call you anytime."

"Don't marry me off so fast. Let's get the bed, a mattress and springs, and go home and eat. Then they'll deliver the bed and mattress and we can try it out," he said, licking his lips and looking at her.

She smiled, shaking her head.

As they drove to the house, he went through what they had already done to the house, what they had lined up to do and what else should be added to the list. "Now I know you need a new roof, and I know a really good roofer. I'll call and get you a couple of estimates."

"Tom, I don't want to pay for all this at once. I have lots of windows. I'm having a security system installed. I've bought a lot of paint. I'll have bills and more bills."

He kept his attention on his driving as he talked. "Em, put all of this on the ranch expenses. We're still married. We're still a couple and we'll pay it out of the ranch budget."

"That simply means you'll pay it all," she said, looking at him in surprise. "You're divorcing me. Why would you pay for all this?"

He reached over with his free hand to squeeze hers. "You're my wife right now, and this divorce is not out of anger. Don't fuss. I'll just add it to the ranch tab. You forget about it."

She was surprised he would do that, but was more lost in his remark about how their divorce was not out of anger. But what difference did that make? They had made mistakes and hurt each other and soon would part.

"You're worrying. Don't. It's taken care of.

Uncle Woody's house, which is now Emily's house, is getting a makeover."

"Thank you, Tom."

He reached over to give her hand another squeeze. "Sure. I intend to do some things right."

"You do a lot of things right," she said. She was amazed that he would do this for her. She rode the last two blocks in silence wondering what Tom really felt and wanted.

When they got home, they had to deal with the first window company. They were so impressed, they decided to skip getting the other estimates and go with this firm.

It was two in the afternoon before they ate lunch and she washed her new sheets. Then they went back to painting. As she painted, her thoughts were on Tom.

He worked fast and efficiently. He'd already taken care of the alarm system. The downstairs windows would be installed in two weeks, which was a rush job for custom-made windows. Going ahead without discussing it, Tom had also hired a professional outfit to paint the outside of the house and they had started this morning. And now he was going to pay all her repair bills.

Tom got things done, and with his help, it was going to take her far less time to finish restoring the house. How long would he stay? Trying to catch Maverick, if it was even possible, could take a long time. So far, she didn't think anyone had come close to learning the true identity of this monster. Maybe she would be the last victim—but how long would Tom feel she might need protection?

In some ways they were getting along better than they had, or maybe she had just relaxed about being with him. She was looking forward to meeting the Valentines Saturday. Tom liked them and his voice softened when he talked about them.

Like shifting sands beneath her feet, she felt as if her world was changing again, slight changes that might make a big difference later. She thought about Tom holding her in the store and telling her she wasn't alone. She expected Tom to eventually get the divorce and they would no longer be in each other's lives. He probably expected to marry again and she was sure he would. He probably expected her to marry again and she was sure she would not. She still wanted the divorce and she was certain he did. As great as Tom was, they could not have happiness together. Tom needed a family, and she couldn't give him his own kids.

The following day after the store delivered the bed, she got out her new sheets and Tom helped. He wore cutoffs, boots and another T-shirt with the sleeves ripped away, and it kept her tingly and physically aware of him every second they were together.

They made the bed and she spread a comforter on top with some new pillows. She stood back to admire it. "I think it's beautiful."

"I agree," he said, picking her up. His voice had lowered. "Let's try it out. I've been waiting for this moment."

"Aw, Tom, don't get me all torn up when I'm getting over what we went through," she said, but at the same time, joy rocked her and she loved being in his arms.

She put her arm around his neck and he carried her to the bed, placing his knee on the mattress to lower her. While she wanted to kiss him, she didn't want to get tied up in emotional knots again. "Tom, we can't do this."

"Sure, we can. Try me and see," he said, stretching beside her and holding her in his arms as his mouth covered hers. She felt as if she were in free fall, the world spinning around her as his tongue stroked hers and he ran his hand over her breast and down to slip beneath her T-shirt. She tightened her arms and thrust her hips against him and felt his hard erection. Pushing aside her bra, he caressed her, his hand warm against her skin.

For a moment, she thought, *just for a moment...* She ran her hands over him, beneath his shirt as he had done, feeling his smooth back, the solid muscles. But she knew she was getting into deep trouble and would get hurt all over again. She slipped out of his embrace and stepped off the bed, shaking her head.

"I can't go through all that pain."

He gazed at her solemnly. She wanted to go right back into his arms, but she knew the futility of that, because it would lead straight to more unhappiness with nothing solved between them.

She turned and went downstairs and outside, trying to find something she could work on far away from him, away from the new bed that had been one more big mistake. The thought of sleeping in a comfortable bed instead of a narrow cot night after night had seemed so marvelous, but a bed and Tom—the mere thought made her hot and tingly.

He still could melt her with a look. She was headed for more heartbreak if she wasn't careful and didn't keep up her guard. Tom was a wonderful, sexy man, but they had no future together. She needed to stay aware of that all the time with him. They had relaxed now and had fun a lot of the time. But with hot sex and fiery passion, she would soon want him back on a permanent basis and then the problem of her inability to have children would come crashing down on her again and Tom would say goodbye.

She returned to her painting, working fast, focusing on her task and trying to avoid thinking about Tom. Then around four o'clock he stepped into the room. She heard his boot heels as he approached the open door and stepped inside.

"How're you doing?"

"Painting away and getting a lot done. You're an inspiration," she said, trying to keep things light and impersonal again, where they seemed to get along the best.

"I'm glad to hear I inspire you. And I'm glad you're okay. Shall I get carryout or do you want to go to a restaurant, or what?"

"I think carryout will be perfect."

"You had your chance to go out to dinner." He turned and was gone and she went back to painting. It was a couple of hours later when he sent her a text that he was leaving and taking orders. Smiling she sent him a reply and kept painting.

Half an hour later, she heard a loud whistle. Startled, she smiled and put down her brush. She went into the hall to look over the banister. He stood below with his hands on his hips and his hair in its usual tangle.

"I'm here and dinner's here, so come on down."

"I have a brush full of paint. You should have given me a warning."

"Bring your brush and I'll take care of it." He turned away without waiting for an answer. Smiling, she picked up her paintbrush and went downstairs.

They ate salads, barbecued ribs and corn bread on the porch and then went back to painting. It wasn't until ten o'clock when they sat back down together on the porch. As usual, she had raspberry tea and he had his cold beer.

"I'm amazed how much you've gotten done. I don't recall you being that fast before."

"I'm getting better as I age."

"Maybe we both are," she said, smiling in the dark.

They sat and talked until midnight and then walked up the stairs together. "Now you sleep tight in your big, cushy new bed while I crawl into my sleeping bag on the floor."

At the top of the stairs as they started down the hall, he put his arm across her shoulders. She smiled. "I will remind you, you insisted on staying here. I told you there was nowhere for you to sleep."

"Not quite true now. If you get lonesome, just whisper. I'll hear you."

She laughed. "Good night, Tom. You can have my cot."

"No, thanks. I'll wait for your invitation." He switched off the lights and she could hear him rustling around and then all was quiet. She suspected it would be a long time before she would get to sleep.

What would it be like when he went back to the ranch and she was in this big old house all by herself? She knew she was going to miss him badly.

In the night a clap of thunder rattled the windows and jolted her awake. She could hear the wind whistling around the house outside and felt the cool breeze coming through the open windows. She got out of bed and slipped on flip-flops to go turn off the attic fan.

Brilliant flashes of lightning illuminated the interior of the room, so she could see as went out into the hall. She bumped into Tom, who steadied her. "Did the thunder wake you?" she asked, aware of his hands still on her arm and waist.

As if to emphasize her words, thunder rumbled again and a flash of lightning cast a silvery brilliance in the hall and was gone, followed by the hiss of a sudden downpour.

"I hoped you'd be scared of thunder and jump into my arms. You can get in my sleeping bag and be cozy."

"Are you trying to wrangle an invitation to sleep in my new bed?"

He ran his finger lightly over her collarbone. "My darlin', if I get an invitation to get on your new bed, I will not sleep. I can think of wonderful ways to try out that new bed." Lightning flashed and she gazed up at him. "Damn, I want you, and it's been a hell of a long time and we're still married." He drew her to him and leaned close to kiss her on the threshold of her bedroom. "You know you want to kiss," he whispered. "Live a little, Em."

Seven

Emily's breath caught as her arms slipped around his neck. Common sense went with the wind. Tom was right. She wanted him, it had been a long time and they were married.

She relished being in his strong arms, held tightly against his virile body that for an hour or two could drive every problem into oblivion.

His hand roamed over her, caressing her breasts, sliding down over her bottom and drifting over her, setting her on fire with wanting him. "Why do we have this effect on each other?" she whispered, more to herself than to him.

"I can't answer your question," he said between

kisses. His tongue followed the curve of her ear and then he tugged away the T-shirt she slept in, drawing it over her head and dropping it to the floor. He cupped her soft breasts in his callused hands while his thumbs caressed her, drawing circles so lightly, making her shake and gasp with pleasure.

"I can't resist you. I never could." She sighed.

He framed her face with his hands. "That's damn mutual. You would have been free of me a long time ago if we could walk away from each other, but we can't. You take my breath away, Em. I dream about you. I still want you even when I should let you go."

She didn't reason out what he said to her. Instead, she kissed him and stopped all conversation. His arms tightened around her and he peeled away her pajama bottoms, tossing them aside while holding her tightly.

It had been too long, aeons, since they had made love, and his body beneath her hands was fit and strong. She wanted that strength, his passion for life, hot kisses and lovemaking that could shut out the pain of loss.

He was an exciting man, and all the things she couldn't be—physically strong, a decorated warrior, tough, sexy. Her world had been caring for her aging uncle, raising her baby, taking pictures of families and children and pets.

For right now, Tom's kisses drove away the heart-breaking problems between them. At the moment nothing was as important as Tom. Making love tonight would not satisfy anything except carnal lust, but she wanted him and he was here with her. If they made love, maybe she could be more relaxed with him, less sexually responsive to even the slightest touch—although that had never happened in the past. Sex with him had always had just the opposite effect, as she knew it would tonight. If they made love, she would want to make love again soon. She would want more instead of less because making love with Tom was fantastic.

She ran her hands over him. Her fingers shook as she peeled away his briefs.

His dark hair was tangled, falling on his forehead. She ran her hands over his broad, muscled shoulders, letting her hand slide down over his flat stomach, his narrow waist.

He was hard, ready to love, and she caressed him, wanting him, wanting to take her time. They hadn't made love in a year and now that they'd started, she couldn't stop and she was certain Tom didn't want to stop. He picked her up and moved to her new bed. He lay down, holding her against him while he stroked and kissed her and moved over her.

He showered kisses on her, starting at her ankle, and then stretched beside her and drew her closer, his leg moving between hers, parting her legs as he caressed her intimately.

She held him tightly, kissing him, the pressure building while desire intensified. Her hips moved and she arched against his hand, straining for release.

His fingers drove her, and then his mouth was on her, his tongue sending her over the edge as she thrashed and burst with release and need for all of him.

She moved over him to kiss him, taking him in her mouth, using her tongue and hands while she rubbed her breasts against him.

With a growl deep in his throat, he rolled her over and moved between her legs to look down at her.

"You're beautiful. I'll be right back," he said, starting to leave.

"I don't need protection," she replied, the moment changing as reality invaded the passionate idyll they had created. "I can't get pregnant, Tom."

He kissed her again, another devastating kiss that made her want him inside her and drove her wild with need. Shifting away swiftly, she got on her knees.

"We're doing this, so let's take our time. I haven't been loved by you in so very long. Take the night and drive away our sorrows. Let's grab joy here and hold it tight. I'm going to make you want me like you never have before," she said, her tongue stroking his thick manhood. "Turn over."

She caressed the backs of his legs, her hands trailing lightly over sculpted, hard muscles. She slowly ran her tongue, hot and wet, up the backs of his thighs, her fingers moving between his legs, her hand playing over his hard butt. Then he rolled back over, pulling her on top of him to kiss her passionately.

As she looked down at him, she wondered why he dazzled her so much and always had. "I can't resist you," she said.

"That's my line," he replied solemnly. "You have it all mixed up—I'm the one who can't resist."

She swung her leg over him to kneel beside him, running her tongue over him again while her fingers stroked and toyed with him. He fondled her breasts, his hands warm, his fingers brushing her nipples. Then he shifted, turning to take her breast in his mouth and run his tongue over the taut peak.

She tried to caress and kiss every inch of him until Tom knelt between her legs, putting her legs on his shoulders, his hands driving her to more heights.

"Come here," she demanded, tugging his hip with one hand, holding his rod with her other. "I want you inside me."

He shifted, coming down to give her a deep kiss that made her heart pound as she clung to him. "Tom, love me. I want you more than you can imagine."

He entered her slowly, filling her and almost withdrawing, moving with slow strokes that drove her wild as she tugged at him. She locked her long legs around his waist, clinging to him, wanting to consume him and for both of them to reach ecstasy and release.

He kissed her as he took his time, driving her wild with need. And then he thrust deep and faster, pumping and taking her with him as tension built until she climaxed, bursting with release, rapture, crying out.

"I love you," she gasped without thought.

Tension gathered swiftly again, built, and she achieved another orgasm. Tom kept up his relentless thrusts, and in minutes, his shuddering release came as she gasped and cried out with another. They clung tightly to each other and gradually her breathing slowed to normal. Then they were finally still, locked in each other's arms.

He showered light kisses on her temple, her ear, her cheek while he finger-combed her long hair away from her face.

Shifting, he held her close and kept her with him as he rolled to his side and faced her, all the while continuing to brush light kisses on her body and lips.

She knew when she let him go and the idyll

ended, their problems would emerge, as omnipres-
ent as ever. The problems they had between them
would last a lifetime. Nothing could take them
away. The moments of lovemaking only briefly
blocked everything else out.

Feeling sadness seep back, she held Tom. She
couldn't give him more children and he didn't want
to stay married.

"You have to be the sexiest man ever."

One corner of his mouth rose in a slight smile.
"I don't think you have a lot of experience to com-
pare, but I'm glad you think that," he said gently.
"Em, there aren't words for how much I wanted
to make love to you."

"We didn't solve anything tonight," she said,
voicing aloud her thoughts. "I don't care. I wanted
you to kiss me. I wanted to make love." He was
damp with sweat, his hair a tangle. She wound her
fingers in it, running them down over the stubble on his jaw. Then her fingers played over the
red lightning bolt tattoo on his right shoulder. She
stroked his back, sliding her hand over his butt,
down to the back of his thigh.

His arm tightened around her waist, pulling her
closer against him. "You're right. It didn't change
anything, but I wanted to hold you and kiss you
again. Let me stay here with you a bit. You have
the rest of your life to get away from me," he said.

And that hurt. Reality was coming back and she couldn't stop it.

"Sure, Tom," she said, holding him, staying in his arms as they remained quiet. She couldn't have regrets for their lovemaking.

She finally shifted slightly. "You can stay here in my bed tonight."

Turning, he drew her against his side. "This seems right in so many ways."

She kissed his shoulder lightly in agreement and felt a pang, wishing they could go back to where they could love each other freely. Where they could feel they were doing right by the other person and their marriage was good. For tonight it was an illusion and she could pretend, but tomorrow, she would have to live with the truth.

He held her close and she clung to him, her arm wrapped around his narrow waist. She wished she could go back a couple of years and have a second chance, because she could see how she had driven Tom away. She ran her finger along his jaw and tried to think about the present, tonight, about loving him and having him in her arms, and forget everything else for now. Tomorrow the problems would all be right there for her to live with and try to cope.

With morning he drew her into his arms to kiss her awake. It was two hours later before they showered together and more than another hour before they went their separate ways to dress.

After breakfast they mopped up where the rain came in last night.

"You have a working alarm system now, in the house and in the yard."

"You've put motion-detector lights all over the place. The door locks all work. If you need to go to the ranch even for just a few days, go ahead."

"If I have to go, I'll tell you. Otherwise, I'm here for a while longer." He turned to face her. "I'll work outside now, so if you want me, I'll be on the east side of the house."

"I'll paint inside," she said and left him.

As Emily painted, she thought about living with Tom.

How would she cope when he walked out of her life? Would they say goodbye and never see each other again? Maybe she would see him at the Texas Cattleman's Club. But if she didn't like living in the old house she had inherited, she would move to Dallas. She would move if she got enough clients and business from the area. If she lived there, she didn't think she would ever see Tom. There were questions about her future that she couldn't answer.

Now, looking around her at the house she had inherited, the smell of fresh paint still filling the air, she thought about her future, when she would have to deal with another parting with Tom. This time a permanent one.

Saturday morning sunshine spilled in through the open windows and Tom was eager to wake Emily. Today was their picnic with the Valentines and he was excited. She'd told him to act as her human alarm clock if she slept past six thirty. It was ten seconds past six thirty now.

He stood beside her bed for seconds, looking at her sleep, her hair spread on the pillow, the sheet down to her waist, her breasts pushing against her T-shirt. He slipped beneath the sheet and pulled her into his arms.

She stirred, wrapped an arm around his neck and rolled over. He couldn't resist. He kissed her. He started out in fun, expecting her to wake instantly, the way she usually did. But the minute he was in bed with her and had her in his arms, all playfulness left him and he wanted to make love to her. He knew he was weaving a web of trouble that would ensnare both of them when they moved on in their lives.

By eleven, after they'd made love, showered, dressed and had breakfast, they were ready to go. Tom was in jeans and a navy T-shirt while she wore capri pants and sandals with a red-white-and-blue-striped cotton blouse. Tom had spent the past half hour packing the truck with provisions

for the picnic. Then they locked up the house, setting the new alarm, and left for Royal's big park
by the Texas Cattleman's Club.

When they got to the park, Tom noticed Emily's
expression as she gazed out the car window. "Look
at all the new trees," she said. "They've replaced a
lot of the ones that were destroyed by the tornado."

"This is a great park. We could have gone to the
Cattleman's Club, but a lot of people there would
have wanted to join us. Another time, that would
be fun, but I want you to meet and get to know the
Valentines when it's just us and them."

Emily had been chatting, but as he wound
slowly alongside a silvery pond toward where he
and Natalie had agreed to meet, she became silent,
and he knew she was remembering the last time
she had been in the park. "This is the way we used
to come when we brought Ryan," she said softly.

Tom glanced at Emily and pain stabbed him.
She had her head turned away from him. He
changed course and drove to a deserted parking
area. He stopped the car, unfastened his seat belt
and placed his hand on her shoulder. He hurt, and
his pain was greater because he knew she felt it,
too. She put her head in her hands. "I'm sorry."

A knot in his throat kept him from answering
and tears burned his eyes. He braced for her to
tell him to leave her alone as he pulled her into his
arms as much as he could in his pickup. She put

her arms around his neck and clung to him, which made him feel better because he had expected her to shove him away.

"I'm sorry, Tom. I thought I could do this without tears. It's a happy occasion and I've looked forward to meeting Natalie and her family and I really mean that—" Emily couldn't finish. She cried while he held her tightly, stroking her head.

"This is the first time I've been back in the park since Ryan was alive," she said between pauses to cry. She spoke so softly he could barely hear her. "We all came here together, remember?"

"I know it, darlin', and I wondered if this would tear you up. I've been here with Natalie and the kids once. This is the main park in Royal and where the Valentines always go. The kids love it here just like Ryan did."

"Then it's a good place to come. I'll be all right in a minute."

"I knew you might have difficulty, and I'm not surprised." He buried his head against her, holding her tightly while she clung to him and they cried. "It hurts like hell, Em, but we don't have a choice. I figure there's a little angel in heaven who loves us as much as we love him."

"Why is life—" She couldn't finish through her tears.

"So damn hard?" he offered. "I don't know. There aren't answers for some questions. When I'm ninety—if I make it that far—I'll cry for my son. As long as I live, I'll miss him."

"I will, too. Why aren't we more of a comfort to each other?"

"I don't know. I guess because that loss is a mountain of sadness and blame and guilt between us. It hurts, so go ahead and cry," he said quietly.

She looked up at him while tears still ran down her cheeks. Tom pulled out a clean, folded handkerchief and dabbed at her cheeks as they gazed at each other.

"You're a comfort to me now. I wish I could be for you, but I can see in your eyes that I'm not."

"Shh, Em. There's a point where it's just too much pain. Over our baby I should have saved. Guys that should have made it home and didn't."

"You just seem to go somewhere where I can't reach you."

He pulled her close again and held her tightly.

She stopped sobbing and became quiet. Raising her head, she wiped her eyes. "I'm making us late."

"If there is anyone on earth who will understand people stopping to grieve, it's Natalie. She and Jeremy were so in love. Take your time. The kids will play and Natalie will be fine. I'll call her. We're only a minute or two from where we're going. She'll understand, believe me." Tom continued to stroke Emily's head lightly, wishing he could do more but knowing he couldn't.

"I'm sorry Natalie is widowed, but I'm glad
we'll be with someone who will understand if I
lose it again. That doesn't usually happen when
I'm out with people, but this is different."

"I know it is, and sometimes the memory of losing Ryan just comes at you out of the blue."

When she shifted to brush a light kiss on his
cheek, he looked down at her. "You're a great guy,
Tom. I've been lucky."

He frowned, studying her intently. "Thanks,
Em. That makes me feel better. We've had some
rough times and we'll have more. I want to help,
not be part of the problem."

She looked straight ahead. "You are a help. We
got through the rough times until now, so hopefully, we'll get through what's ahead," she said.
Her voice held a sad note, and he wondered if she
dreaded the divorce or wished they could go ahead
sooner and get it now.

He put his hand behind her head and pulled her
close to kiss her lightly, tenderly, hoping he con-
veyed the bond he knew they would always have.
Even after they divorced and went their separate
ways, memories of Ryan would always be there
between them.

She moved away from him and he let her go.
"I'm ready. She'll know I've been crying, but you
said she would understand."

"She definitely will, and I told her this might

be tough for you. It was for me the first time I was in the park after the wreck."

"Let's go meet them. I'm pulled together. Thanks for being patient and understanding."

"I feel the same as you do, so it's damn easy to be understanding."

He pulled out and returned to the main drive, winding through the park beneath tall oaks until he got to another parking spot near the pond, where a picnic table was already spread.

"There they are—including their dog," Tom said. "Miss Molly is a well-trained golden retriever and as long as we're the only folks out here, she's okay running free, because she sticks close to the kids. She loves those kids. If other families come out, Natalie has a lead she can put Miss Molly on.

"I told you about Colby. He's standoffish, but he'll warm up. He knows me well now, so he's usually responsive around me. I try to not push him," Tom said as he parked. "They're really great kids."

Emily lightly placed her hand on his arm. "You sound happy. You like being with a family and kids. That's what you need, Tom, your own family, your own kids. The sooner we divorce, the sooner you'll have that life."

Frowning slightly, he parked and studied her. "If you marry again, would you be willing to adopt a child?"

"I've never thought about that. I suppose I

would, because the only reason I didn't want to with us was I wanted another Ryan for you," she replied. "The only way we could have a child who would be like you would be if you fathered the child. That's why I held out to not adopt. I kept expecting to get pregnant. If I marry someone else—that wouldn't matter, so yes, I'd adopt."

He had decided long ago they would each be better off if they divorced. Now he knew they would. Emily would have a family and the life she wanted.

He needed to call Nathan and see if they had found any more clues about Maverick. Because Tom felt more strongly than ever that he needed to get out of Emily's life.

Eight

Emily got out when Tom did and they both gathered all they picnic supplies they could handle. Tom carried a big cooler loaded with ice and bottled drinks. He slung a tote bag on his shoulder, with pinwheels and kites sticking out of it. Emily carried a big sack with two beach balls. Two little wooden flutes were in the bottom of the sack. Tom also had an electronic toy for Colby and a little box containing a tiara, a feather boa, bangles and a beaded purse for Lexie to play dress-up. Before he picked up the cooler, he waved and Natalie waved back.

Miss Molly saw them and came bounding over.

She went to Tom, but was too well behaved to jump all over him. He put down everything he carried to pet her and scratch her ears. It was obvious the dog loved him and it was mutual. She looked at Emily, who held her hand out, and Tom stepped closer to her. "Here's Miss Molly. She's friendly and has been through obedience school, so she's well trained."

Miss Molly sniffed Emily's hand and looked up expectantly. Tom took a doggie treat from his pocket and handed it to Emily. "Give her this and she will love you forever."

"That's a bribe."

"And it works beautifully. Try," he said.

She held out the treat, which Miss Molly politely took and ate, wagging her tail. She moved closer and looked up at Emily expectantly.

"See, you have a friend now," Tom said, picking things up to carry to the picnic spot.

Emily smiled as she petted Miss Molly and retrieved what she had been carrying. Miss Molly ran to catch up with Tom and walk beside him, moving around to his left side.

Natalie was sitting at the picnic table with a little redheaded girl on her lap. "Lexie is a little doll," Tom said. "At two, Lexie is too young for outdoor games, so I brought some toys and musical instruments. And I have two beach balls and two kites, but we'll need more wind than this. I have some pinwheels, too."

"You're a walking toy store. No wonder they're excited to see you."

As they drew close, Natalie set Lexie on the ground. The minute her feet touched the grass, she ran with her arms out. Tom put down his things and scooped her up, laughing as he said hello. He looked around and walked over to pick up Colby with the other arm. "Hi, Colby," he said easily. "Isn't this fun? We're at the park and I brought some toys and some things to do." The children were both talking to him and he laughed, setting them on their feet.

"Wait a minute. I need to mind my manners. We have someone new with us. Emily, meet Lexie and Colby. This is my wife, Miss Emily to you two." He looked at Emily. "Lexie's still a toddler, so no telling what you'll be called."

"Whatever she settles on, it'll be fine."

Emily greeted them with a smile while they politely said hello. She barely heard Colby, who shyly looked away.

"We'll get to what I brought, but first, I want to talk to your mama," Tom told them.

As they approached the picnic table, which already had a red-and-white-checkered plastic tablecloth covering it, Emily saw Natalie Valentine turn and come forward to greet them, smiling.

"Emily, I'm Natalie. I'm glad to finally meet you."

"I'm glad to meet you," Emily answered politely, amazed Tom hadn't fallen in love with Natalie, who was pretty with huge green eyes.

Natalie held out her hands. "Let me carry something."

"Here's a cake you can carry," Emily said, handing a covered pan to the other woman.

"Lexie woke up an hour earlier than usual this morning because she was so excited about the picnic today. The kids love to see Tom. He's wonderful with them and he's good to share his time. Jeremy picked the right guy to be friends with, and I know why."

"He's good with kids," Emily said, watching him hunker down to let Lexie and Colby look in the sack he'd brought and pull something out. They each got a pinwheel and stepped away to swing them through the air and make them spin. It was obvious they had played with them before.

"Tom has been a lifesaver for us," Natalie continued. "Last month he installed two new motion-detector lights outside at the B and B. And then I had an appointment to take Colby to the dentist and Miss Molly had an appointment at the groomer at the same time—both hard to change—so Tom took Lexie with him to get Miss Molly to be groomed while I took Colby to the dentist. He

even took Lexie to the pediatrician when she had
to get a tetanus shot because she cut her foot on a
rusty piece of metal. He held her hand while she
got her shot, took her for ice cream and then to
the bookstore."

Emily continued to listen to Natalie talk about
how much Tom had helped her. She was so effu-
sive in her praise for Tom, talking about all the
things he had done for her and her family, that
Emily realized she had pushed Tom away and
hadn't let him take care of her when that was probably what he needed to do.

It was what he was doing now, but she had been
fighting him on it every step of the way, while
Natalie accepted his help and was grateful for it.

In the past Emily had robbed him of his need
to be her protector, a need she decided after listening to Natalie that was as essential to his life
force as breathing. He had tried in the days after
they lost Ryan, but she had wrapped herself in a
shell and withdrawn from him. She hadn't relied
on him then and she wouldn't have now, but he'd
simply taken charge because of worrying about
what Maverick might be intending to do.

She thought about Tom telling her that he had
lost Ryan, but he wasn't going to lose her to a troll.

She watched him with the kids and wondered if
part of the reason they were getting along so much
better now was because he felt he was helping her

and doing things for her. If so, she had made really big mistakes by shutting him out of parts of her life after Ryan's death.

"I know you and Tom have been estranged in the past," Natalie said quietly. "I don't want to intrude, but it looks as if you might be getting back together. I just want to say you have a wonderful husband who has been so good to us and a marvelous substitute for Jeremy with the kids."

"Tom loves kids. He's got six nieces and nephews, but this past year we haven't seen them often, because all three of his brothers have moved farther away."

"Jeremy picked well when he got Tom for a friend. But Tom's gone through a lot at home and abroad. Jeremy told me about some of what they did and it was rough. Tom's a tough guy, but losing his son has really been hard on him. Just as I know it's hard on you. That's something we all share. But enough about our lives."

As Emily started to unpack the things they'd carried from the car, her thoughts were on all Natalie had said.

The more Emily thought about it, the more she realized that pushing Tom away after Ryan's death, doing things herself and shutting him out had been disastrous. But now she was accepting his help, and they both seemed to be thriving. He was getting the house in shape far faster than she would have been able to do. And since Tom appeared, she hadn't had any more messages from Maverick.

At least this part was good. She was happy to meet Natalie and the kids, who'd made her realize that it would have helped Tom heal more after they lost Ryan if she hadn't shut him out. He needed her to rely on him, to need him—which was something he had found with the Valentines.

Emily wondered if it was too late for her. Was having Tom working on Uncle Woody's house and staying with her for protection enough to meet the need he had to be a provider in her life and in the marriage?

Natalie watched as the kids played with the beach balls. Tom patiently helped Lexie, who was too little to keep up with her brother or do much of anything with her beach ball except toss it around and let Tom bring it back and roll it to her.

As soon as Emily and Natalie were done unpacking everything, the kids started dancing around Tom, asking him to create bubbles for them to pop.

"They'll keep him busy," Natalie said, turning to look at Emily. "Tom told me about the hateful email you got. It's terrible, but I'm so glad you two got it straightened out between you." She gave a faint smile and shook her head. "Tom's secret family. He is so good to us. I would have been sick if I thought all he's done for us would cause you both pain. Tom is a wonderful person."

"Yes, he is, and he thought your husband was. He told me about Jeremy, but that was a while ago. When I saw that picture, I didn't put it together and think about your husband. I just accepted the email as truth."

"I hope they catch this person before someone else gets hurt."

"I hope so, too. I'm sorry, Natalie, about Jeremy. Tom thought so much of him."

"Thanks," Natalie said. "I'm sorry for your loss. Tom is good to always spend time with the kids. Both kids love him. He's so patient with them and good for Colby."

"He's good with kids because he really likes them," Emily said quietly, hurting as she watched Tom play with Lexie and Colby. "And he's patient," she said, thinking again if she could have gotten pregnant, they might not be getting the divorce. Tom had been wonderful with Ryan.

"We've both lost so much," Natalie said quietly. "I hope you and Tom can work things out, because he should have his own family, his own kids."

"I agree with you about that and I know we have a mutual bond in losing someone we love deeply." She looked around. "We better start getting food ready, or there will be other kinds of tears shed."

"Indeed, there will be," Natalie said, smiling.

"Before you and Tom arrived, they were coming to me every five minutes to ask when you'd get here and how soon we'll eat. Let's get some of this set up and then we can go join them and play for a short time. If you don't want to, that's okay," Natalie said.

"It'll be fun. Look at Tom. He has to be having a good time."

They paused a moment and watched Tom open a bottle, dip a wand inside and then wave it, leaving a stream of big bubbles. Laughing, both kids began to chase and pop bubbles while Tom kept producing more.

Another pang struck Emily as she looked at Tom. Wind tangled his hair. He was agile and strong, playing with the kids and obviously enjoying it. This was a fun few hours, but their lives were not a constant picnic with kids included. Their marriage was over and that was one more thing she had to accept and learn to live with. Tom was handsome, so appealing—she turned from watching him, focusing on the kids and laughing at their antics.

"Your children are wonderful."

"Thank you," Natalie answered. "They have their moments, and Colby has special needs and special abilities. They're good kids and I love them with all my heart."

Looking at both kids, Emily hurt because she

wanted her own. She wanted to run and join the fun and play with them, too, but she didn't want to leave Natalie and they didn't need three adults mixing with the bubbles. "Lexie is so cute."

Natalie laughed. "She thinks so. She would love to have my shoes and makeup. I can't imagine what I'm in for when she's a teen."

Emily smiled. Tom glanced their way and said something to Colby and Lexie. He turned to walk toward Emily and Natalie.

"Hey, when do we get to eat around here?"

"We can any time you want to fire up that grill and do burgers," Natalie said.

"I'll tell Colby and Lexie and go to work at the grill."

"I'll tell them," Natalie said. "You get the food. Emily and I can play with them while you cook. I think we have everything else out and ready."

"Good deal," he answered.

Emily spread a blanket and gave each child a new box of crayons and tablets of plain paper so they could draw.

Natalie joined her and after a few minutes, Emily left to help Tom with the cooking and getting last-minute things on the table.

When they all sat down to eat, she felt as if she were part of the family. Natalie was easy to get to know and Emily already loved the kids. Colby was quiet, sometimes a little withdrawn, but he liked all the toys and gadgets Tom had brought. She took pictures of them and of everybody.

They had homemade strawberry ice cream for dessert along with chocolate chip cookies Natalie had made. As they sat in the shade and ate ice cream and cookies, Miss Molly stretched out at Tom's feet. Tom ran the toe of his boot back and forth behind her ear and she looked serenely happy.

When they put things away after the picnic, Lexie ran up to grab Tom's hand and tug. Colby stood back, holding one of the beach balls. "Back to work," Tom said, getting up to join the kids again. "Don't carry anything to the cars. I can do that later."

"I'll go with you," Emily said, smiling at Natalie. "Take a break and sit in the shade. We'll play with Lexie and Colby. It'll be fun."

Natalie smiled. "Thanks. Stop whenever you've had enough."

Tom and Colby moved yards apart while Emily stood near Lexie, who was too little to play but wanted to participate. The adults tossed the beach ball first to one child and then the other. Lexie couldn't catch it, but she chased it to bat it and Emily helped.

By late afternoon, Lexie was sitting on a blanket alternately playing with a doll and drawing while Colby played with the electronic game that

Tom had brought. The three adults sat in the shade and talked.

Emily enjoyed being with all of the Valentines. Lexie brought over her drawing and scrambled up onto her lap. Emily held her, admiring her drawing and talking to her about making another picture. The minute she climbed on her lap, Emily thought of Ryan. She looked down at Lexie's red hair, thinking she was an adorable child. She took the crayons to draw. As she drew, Lexie listened attentively while Emily made up first one story and then another to go with the pictures. When she finished, she asked Lexie to draw a story and watched and listened as the little girl spoke of a mouse and an elephant and drew unrecognizable creatures. But she was happy with her story and her drawings.

"Emily, you don't have to do that the rest of the evening," Natalie said, smiling. "I think you've served your time."

Shaking her head, Emily smiled. "I'm having a good time, too. As long as she wants to. When I want to stop, I will."

Lexie tugged on her hand. "Let's do another one," she said.

"Do you want to tell another story?" Emily asked, looking at Lexie and thinking how wonderful it was to have a little child in her lap again.

Lexie's eyes sparkled as she nodded. "I have a story about a kitty and a butterfly."

Emily listened, smiling and smoothing Lexie's hair, thinking Natalie had a wonderful family. She glanced up to see Tom watching her. Their gazes met and she wondered what he was thinking.

The sun was below the treetops in the west when Natalie announced they needed to pack things up and get home. She called to Miss Molly, and the big dog loped to her side.

"We'll follow you home and I can help carry things inside," Tom said.

"You don't need to do that," she said, smiling at him. "Emily told me how you're helping her get her house painted. I know how big a job that can be. Besides, I have four couples at the bed-and-breakfast, just getting away from city life for a weekend. The guys carried the things out for me this morning and have already told me they would carry the stuff in when I get back. Their reward will be the strawberry ice cream," she said, smiling at them.

"Come see me," Lexie said, taking Emily's hand. Her tiny hand felt so small, and Emily's heart lurched when she thought about Ryan holding her hand.

"I'd love to see your room and Colby's, too," Emily said, and Lexie's smile broadened.

"We'll be happy to have you come visit," Natalie said.

They let Miss Molly jump into the back of the SUV and then the kids climbed in and buckled into their car seats, with Natalie checking on Lexie's. Natalie got into the front and Tom closed her door.

Tom draped his arm across Emily's shoulders as they walked to the pickup. She wondered if he even gave any thought to what he was doing, but she was aware of it. The minute he put his arm across her shoulders, she was reminded of old times with him. And then she became aware of how close they were. All day he had looked virile, filled with energy, strong and incredibly appealing to her. How much would it tear her up to go back to the house and sleep with him? The thought of making love tonight made her draw a deep breath; she just couldn't suppress her eagerness.

Tom held the pickup door open and she climbed inside. He got in and waited while Natalie backed out and turned to drive away. Then he followed.

"They look like the all-American family, Tom. Especially with the dog hanging out the window," Emily said.

"Except the all-American dad was shot dead on foreign soil, defending his country so we can go on picnics. He's not in that car with his wife and kids and dog."

Emily wanted to reach for Tom's hand, just

to hold it. At one time in her life that's what she would have done, but not now. Now they were going their separate ways soon and reaching for him would be almost like reaching to hold a stranger's hand. "You knew that when you joined the service," she said.

"I know I did, but sometimes when I'm with Natalie and the kids, it gets to me, because Jeremy should be with them instead of me."

"You've really kept your promise to Jeremy. She's so grateful for all you've done for them."

"I'm trying," he said. "When I think of the sacrifice he made, there's never enough I can do."

"You're a good guy," Emily said, and meant it. Tears threatened because she had lost Tom and there were moments it hurt badly. After a few minutes, she pulled herself together. "Natalie appreciates everything you've done and it's obvious the kids love you. You should have your own kids," she said quietly. He shot her a quick, startled glance but said nothing.

She felt another wave of sadness that she couldn't give Tom another little boy. If only she had been able to get pregnant, they might have had a chance to save their marriage. But that wasn't what had happened.

"They are cute kids. Lexie knows she is," Tom said, smiling. "That little girl can steal the show when she wants to. I'm glad you and Natalie met. I should have done that long ago, but you and I have been out of each other's lives for a long time now."

"I'm glad to meet her. I understand her loss and she understands mine—actually, ours."

"Yes. She's done well, but she has moments. She keeps a good front for the kids' sakes, so that helps in a way."

Emily thought about how all three of them— she, Natalie and Tom—had been targets of Maverick in a way. But Maverick's hateful lies had backfired, bringing them closer together instead of driving them all apart.

When they got back to her house, she was astonished again by the difference only a week had made. The new coat of paint was beginning to transform the house into the home she remembered and loved and always thought was so beautiful. Tom had started working on the yard because the days were getting warmer. He'd made two beds ready for spring planting. Filled with energy, Tom got things done, but she always had been impressed by his strength and vigor.

"It's just been a week and you've made a giant difference. It doesn't look like the same house."

"I'm glad you noticed, and you sound happy with it."

"I am happy with it. It's done and it looks nice and thank you."

"Good. It's a hell of a lot safer and more secure, too," Tom said. He parked at the side of the house, leaving the pickup so it could be seen from the street.

"You're not getting out of the pickup," she said, looking at him sitting still, staring straight ahead.

"No, I'm looking at the garage."

"Oh, heavens, what now, Tom? There must be something I need to fix."

"There sure as hell is. Emily, that garage is as old as this house. That big mulberry tree with giant roots is pushing the garage over and the driveway up."

"You want me to get rid of the garage?"

"Yes. You need to get estimates—I'll do it—on a new driveway and a new garage and come into this century. Or even come into the last half of the last century. That thing is simply going to collapse someday soon and you don't want to be in it when it does."

She looked at the old garage and the cracked slabs of concrete driveway that had been pushed several inches into the air.

"Do you remember when your uncle Woody stopped using it?" Tom asked.

"I was probably about twelve. Okay. You're right about the garage."

Tom smiled. "So I'm finally right about something concerning this house."

"You're right about everything concerning this

house. Tom, it is definitely better. It would have taken me months to get done what you've done. I'm grateful for your help," she said.

"I'll get your estimates on a driveway and the cost for a new garage. This will be a garage today's car will fit into," he said, grinning and shaking his head. "That thing was built for a Model T."

Together they carried the picnic things into the house. "It's a pretty Saturday night," he remarked. "After we get through putting the stuff away, let's sit on the porch, have a drink and enjoy the evening."

"Sure," she said, knowing if they did that many more times, she would miss having him here when he returned to the ranch. "But I need a shower first—I've been outside all day, in the grass, petting the dog—"

"Right. I know one thing that would make taking a shower better—"

"It's not going to happen tonight."

He grinned. "I have to keep trying. I can really be fun to take a shower with, or maybe you remember. I remember you're lots of fun to shower with. It would make this a superspecial Saturday."

"Will you stop?" she said, laughing and shaking her head. "No, we don't shower together. What would you like to drink? Let me guess—a cold beer."

"Ah, you know me too well. All the mystery is gone."

"There's plenty of mystery about you—I'm surprised you haven't fallen in love with Natalie Valentine. She is so sweet and has a wonderful family. And you love that dog."

He came back to put his hands on her shoulders and she wondered what chord she had struck. Was he falling in love with Natalie? She gazed into his seductive hazel eyes.

"I'll tell you what, darlin'. I don't fall in love with someone because of their dog. Or their kids—and those are adorable kids. Natalie is beautiful, but she's Jeremy's widow and she still loves him. And he was my buddy."

"You're a good guy, Tom," she said, turning back to her task.

When they were done putting things away in the kitchen, she turned to him. "I'm going upstairs to shower—alone. I'll meet you on the porch. The first one done can get drinks. See you in thirty minutes."

"Fine. I'll go upstairs and shower, too." At the head of the stairs he turned to her. "The invitation is still open."

"I'll have to admit, I'm tempted—"

"Oh, darlin'," he said, holding his arms out. "Come join me. We'll have a shower you'll never forget." She laughed and he laughed with her. "See,

I told you I can be fun in the shower," he said. "We're not even there yet and I have you laughing."

"You are fun, you devil," she said, squeezing his jaw and looking into his mischievous eyes. "As fun as you are, I'm going to shower all by myself and then enjoy sitting with you on the porch," she said.

He placed his arms casually on her shoulders. "We can still enjoy each other's company. It's been a good day."

"It has. The Valentines are wonderful."

"Yes, they are, but the good time today wasn't just because of the Valentines. You and I can laugh and enjoy each other. We haven't totally lost it," he said with so much confidence she felt a thrill.

"I know we can as long as we stay away from real life and the serious stuff."

"I'll settle for what we can get. We can do a lot of things together," he said, his voice changing, becoming deeper while his hands slid down to rub her bare arms lightly.

"I know we can."

Her heartbeat raced as his gaze lowered to her mouth. Her lips parted.

"Tom," she whispered, his name an invitation. She might have huge regrets very soon, but at this moment she wanted to kiss him. What would one kiss hurt?

When his mouth covered hers, she opened to him and felt on fire. Their tongues mingled as he wrapped his arm around her and pulled her tightly against him. She hugged him around his waist and ran one hand over his muscled back.

She had no idea how long they kissed, but when she felt his hand on her breast, she placed her hand over his. "Wait," she whispered, looking up at him. "I want to shower and sit on the porch and talk and maybe kiss again—okay?"

He inhaled deeply and nodded. "Okay." He caressed her nape and tugged lightly on her braid. "Take your hair down."

"I will. I'll see you on the porch." She walked away, hearing his boots as he went into the room where he kept his things. Now what would she agree to after her shower? She better think before she brought pain and regret crashing back down on them.

When she came down, he was already on the porch. She wore navy capri pants, flip-flops, a pale blue sleeveless cotton blouse and a clip in her hair to hold it behind her head. The minute he saw her, Tom stood up. His gaze drifted over her from her head to her toes, making her tingle. She took in tight jeans, his black boots and short-sleeved navy T-shirt. To her, he was still the most handsome man she knew. And definitely the sexiest. She strolled to the empty chair beside him and picked up the drink he'd prepared for her.

He stepped closer and smiled at her, making her heart race as she gazed into his eyes. "You look as good as a million dollars."

"Thank you. You look rather good yourself." She didn't want to admit how appealing he did look to her.

"Let's fix this," he said, reaching over to take the clip out of her hair and placing it on the table. She smiled at him as she shook her head, letting her hair fan out over her shoulders.

As they rocked and talked, she felt as if she was standing on the edge of a high cliff and a misstep could mean ruin. She thought about what she should do and what she wanted to do. She wanted to be in his arms, making love again. How much would that hurt later? It wouldn't change anything. It just might mean more heartache.

"Think you'll stay in Royal or move to Dallas after our divorce?" he asked after a long silence.

"Right now, after a fun day together, I don't want to think about the divorce." She gazed into the darkness and sipped her tea. "I'll probably stay in this area unless some opportunity with my photography comes up and causes me to move on. We'll cross paths, I'm sure."

With his feet propped on another chair, Tom was silent. While he sipped his beer, he idly rubbed one knee and she remembered how he ran and played with the kids. She also remembered how badly his knee was hurt in the bus wreck and the big scar he still carried.

"Does your knee hurt?"

He looked around. "Not really. I guess rubbing it sometimes has gotten to be a habit from when it did hurt."

"That's good. It used to bother you some after a long day like today," she said.

"I don't think about it much any longer. We'll both carry that night with us in our memories forever, but the pain isn't as constant as it was."

"I agree. I'm sorry that you got hurt so badly. I was scared I'd lose you both," she said, thinking about all they had been through.

"I'm sorry I made it and Ryan didn't," he said quietly.

"Tom, don't ever apologize because you survived," she said, turning to stare at him. "I didn't want to lose either one of you," she said. "I was terrified when they told me you were on the critical list along with Ryan. I called your brother and that's why you were on so many prayer lists, because he got the word out. Don't ever apologize for surviving."

"I figured you wished I had died instead of Ryan," Tom replied. Stunned, she stared at him in the darkness while she clutched his hand.

Nine

"If one of us could have lived and one couldn't, I would rather it had been Ryan, too," Tom continued.

Shocked, she shook her head. "Tom, I never felt that way," she said, staring at him in the dark. "That's dreadful. I never for one second wanted to lose you."

He didn't answer and she wondered if he doubted her. "It has never occurred to me you could have thought I wished it had been you. I loved you. I loved you so much." When he still didn't answer her, she hurt to think he had been carrying that idea around all this time. "I was so scared you wouldn't make it. I stayed awake all through that first night praying for you and Ryan."

Setting her glass of tea aside, she got up and stepped over to sit in his lap. She framed his face with her hands so she could look into his eyes even though it was dark on the porch. "I never wished you had died instead of Ryan. Not for one part of a second. Oh, how I loved you."

His arms tightened around her and he shifted, cradling her against his shoulder as he leaned over to kiss her, a possessive kiss that made her insides seize up. She kissed him back as if she could erase all the heartaches and differences with their kiss. She leaned away again and cupped his chin in her hand.

"Don't ever think or say that again. With my whole heart I wanted you and Ryan, both of you, to survive." Holding him tightly, she resumed their kiss.

Minutes later, she raised her head. "Tom, I never for one second wanted you to die," she said.

He gazed intently at her and started to say something, but she stood, taking his hand. She pulled lightly and he came to his feet to sweep her into his arms.

If she couldn't convince him with words, she wanted to show him with her loving, with kisses and caresses to give him all the sensual pleasure possible. As if he knew what she wanted, he carried her inside. Holding her close, he climbed the staircase and switched on the light in the upstairs hall.

In her bedroom beside the new bed, he stood her on her feet and kissed her. The instant his mouth covered hers, she trembled with desire. She stepped back to take off her blouse, moving slowly while he watched her. When she had her blouse off, she stepped forward to pull off his shirt and rake her hands over his chest and shower kisses there, running her tongue over the flat, hard nipples, tangling her fingers in his thick chest curls.

He caressed her breasts, cupping them and stroking her nipples lightly with his thumbs while she peeled away her capri pants. She unfastened and pulled off his belt as they kissed. Then she unfastened his jeans and pushed them down his legs.

Tom paused to kick off his boots and pull off the rest of his clothes and her lace panties. He placed his hands on her hips and stepped back to look at her. "You're beautiful. I've dreamed about you and spent hours remembering." His fingers again drifted over her breast, a faint brush of his hand that was as electrifying as his hungry gaze.

His look was as sexy and stimulating as his touch, making her quiver. She twisted and turned, rubbing her warm, naked body against him, all the while caressing him, touching him, stroking his thick manhood.

"Ah, Em, this is good with you, so good." He leaned down to take her nipple in his mouth and circle the tip with his tongue. Intense sensation shot through her from each hot brush of his tongue and she gasped with pleasure.

"Tom, my love," she whispered. Her fingers trailed over his scars, some new, most old and familiar. She followed with her tongue.

Reaching for her, he watched her expression as he cupped her breasts again.

She clung to his shoulders, closing her eyes and drowning in sensation. "I want to take all night to give you pleasure, to show you how wrong you were."

He kissed her fiercely, holding her tightly as if it might be their last kiss, and she clung to him.

When he released her, he gazed into her eyes. "Tonight is for memories of the good times, for a day well spent, to celebrate being alive."

Emily tangled her fingers in his chest hair as she kissed him. He stood with his eyes closed as she knelt to lick and kiss and stroke him, until he picked her up and placed her on the bed. He propped himself up on an elbow beside her, watching her, and then leaned down to shower kisses and caresses over every inch of her.

He pushed her over onto her stomach, his tongue trailing down her spine, over her smooth, round bottom, lower between her legs and then over the backs of her legs while his hands were everywhere caressing her.

She moaned softly, her hands knotted in the sheets on the bed. She turned to face him, her gaze raking over his muscled body and thick manhood. He stretched out beside her to pull her into his arms and kiss her hard while his hand was warm between her legs, rubbing her, driving her to new heights. She arched against him and ran her hand over his legs, over his thick rod that was hot and hard and ready for her.

With a murmur deep in his throat, he stepped off the bed and picked her up. They looked into each other's eyes while he pulled her up onto her toes. He looked fierce, desire blazing in his expression.

As he kissed her, he braced himself. She locked her long legs around his waist and he lowered her onto his thick shaft.

Gasping with pleasure, she dug her nails into his muscled shoulders and then wrapped her arms around him, clinging tightly to him She wanted his lovemaking to drive her to oblivion, to make love until pain and hurt and loss were mere shadows that couldn't affect her.

And then all thought was gone as she rode him. He thrust hard and fast, driving her to a brink and then over. She cried out with ecstasy before kissing him again, a kiss of love, of longing and of rapture.

Time and hurt didn't exist. She was wrapped in his arms, one with him, and for this moment it felt as if she was enveloped in his love once again.

When she finally slid down to stand, she gazed into his eyes that looked filled with love. For this moment they had recaptured the past. Gently, he picked her up to place her on the bed and stretched out beside her. She lay in his arms, exhausted, pressed against his hard length. Tom held her close against him, slowly combing his fingers through her hair. "This is good, Em," he said in a raspy tone.

She placed her hand on his cheek. They lay quietly, holding each other, touching, stroking each other gently, and she wished the night would stretch into eternity.

"We're way ahead of the schedule for fixing the house, aren't we?" he asked, his deep voice soft in the silent night.

"Yes, thanks to you and your dynamo energy."

"How about going to the ranch for a few days to get a break? You've already blocked off time from your photography. Honestly, I can use a little time on the ranch. Would you do that? A little break won't hurt."

She gazed at him as she thought it over. "Just a few days?"

"Sure. Just a break. I think we've earned one.

I've hired a company to get these hardwood floors back in shape for you."

"Tom—you didn't tell me. Are they putting in new floors?"

"No. It's a cleanup and polish, that sort of thing. If you want something more, though, now is the time to say so."

"No, that will be wonderful. That's all I intended to do. Thank you."

"You're welcome. Let's go to the ranch tomorrow and I'll call and tell them to come do the floors. I know the guy that owns the company, and we can trust him with the house key."

She laughed. "Sure. What's to steal here?" she asked, looking around at an empty room. "Very well. Yes, I'll go to the ranch—what? A week, four days, two days?"

"How is four days?"

"Four days it is. Thanks. I'll make arrangements and we'll go after lunch.

"Where are we staying?"

He leaned close. "Let's try the main house together. Our house. I can stay in a separate bedroom if you want, but four days—let's try, Em."

"You can always get your way with me. You know all you have to do is look at me, touch me or even just stand close and I'm putty."

"Very sexy putty, I'd say."

"Don't try to butter me up now," she said, smiling at him.

"Ah, butter. That's something we haven't tried. Maybe I will butter you up one night."

She laughed and hugged him. "Why can't it stay this way?"

"I can't answer that one."

The next afternoon, they were packed, had the house locked up and were in the car by two o'clock. On the ride back to the ranch, they reminisced about their high school days and dating. Emily wondered if they could maintain their relaxed, friendly attitude on the ranch, where so many painful memories came up day after day.

She would soon know. They moved into the big house and she had a chill run down her spine because she had a feeling they were making a big mistake by coming back when they didn't have to. Standing in the entryway beneath the Waterford crystal chandelier, she looked around.

"Tom, I'll take the guest bedroom on the far west side."

"Good idea. I'll take the one next to it unless you'll just let me move in with you from the start."

She laughed. "Let's see how we're doing by nightfall. We don't have a good track record in this house."

He took her hand and stepped close in front

of her. With his other hand he caressed her nape lightly. "We had the best track record possible until that bus wreck. That's when it all went to hell. But we've been doing pretty well together in town these past weeks."

She nodded but still had the feeling of foreboding.

"I need to go see Gus and check on some things. I'm sure you can entertain yourself, and if nothing else, just take a four-day vacation."

"That sounds awesome," she said, smiling at him. "You get going and my vacation will start. I may go swim."

"Better check the pool over first for critters. No one has been here except a skeleton garden and cleaning staff."

"Oh, yes. I look before I jump in."

"So you do." He smiled at her. "See, we're doing pretty well. Kiss me and we'll see if we are still speaking to each other."

She laughed, but she really didn't feel lighthearted. He stepped close to embrace and kiss her, startling her for one second, and then she held him and returned his kiss, wondering if he would still want to kiss her in four days.

In minutes, he picked her up and carried her to a downstairs bedroom, setting her down only to yank the covers off the bed.

"Tom—" she protested.

"We're alone. What I'm going to do can wait.
This can't," he rasped. In seconds, their clothing
was gone and he picked her up as he kissed her.
She locked her legs around him and he spread his
feet apart, letting her slide down on his thick rod
while they kissed.

Emily held him tightly, moving on him, her cries
of ecstasy smothered by his kisses. She moved fast
with him as he thrust deeply and groaned when he
reached a shuddering climax.

She finally sagged against him, placing her
head on his shoulder as he placed her in bed and
then stretched out beside her.

"You are fantastic and leave me frazzled and in
paradise at the same time."

She smiled. "You're never frazzled. We'll shower
soon, but for a minute I want you close to me. This
is a good way to start our current life here."

They talked softly, stroking each other, and he
seemed to enjoy the moment as much as she did
until he finally rolled over.

"I hate to go, but I have several things to do.
First I'm going to talk to Gus. Then I'm going to
my office in the guesthouse, because I need to
find some old records for our accountant to do
the taxes. No one will be here today except me,
so do whatever you want. We should have dinners
in the freezer and a couple in the fridge. I won't
be gone long."

"I hope not. I don't do well in this big house by myself."

Something flickered in his gaze. "We had a lot of good years here and really good memories. We both need to try to remember to hang on to those times."

She leaned close to kiss him tenderly. "You've been my world since I was sixteen. Then, when the crash happened—"

"A day at a time," he said solemnly. "I'm going to shower and see you later. You find something in that freezer to thaw for us."

"Sure will." She watched him get up and leave the room. He was naked, handsome, all muscle. He had scars, but she barely noticed them. Desire stirred and she wondered if there was any hope for them to have a future together. Was the sex between them blinding them to the problems they faced—or was it helping to work those problems out?

Sex for them had always been good, but they couldn't stay married on that alone, and they really hadn't solved any problems between them. Or had they? There was her discovery that Tom thought she wished he had died instead of Ryan. They'd been able to clear the air about that. And she realized how tense and uptight she had been about getting pregnant, and how that might have driven him away from her. So maybe they were making progress.

After she showered and dressed, she walked through the house, closing off some rooms because she wanted to avoid seeing them.

As she set a casserole out to thaw, she received a call and didn't recognize the number, but then she saw the name Jason Nash on the caller ID and her breath caught.

She answered the call and heard a lilting female voice. "May I please speak to Emily Knox?"

"This is Emily Knox," Emily answered, barely able to catch her breath and feeling as if her heart was being squeezed by a giant fist. She gulped air, trying to calm.

"Mrs. Knox, this is Becky Nash. I'm Polly's mother. I'm sure you remember us."

"Yes, I do," she said, instantly recalling the discussion with the doctor who'd first told them about the Nash family after the bus accident. "How is Polly?" Emily asked, holding her breath and wondering why she was receiving this call.

"Polly is fine," Becky Nash said. "We'll be passing through Texas, and we thought we could stop by if you would like to meet our daughter."

For a moment Emily couldn't answer. Tears filled her eyes and she felt a mixture of emotions—dread at revisiting all the pain from those days when Ryan was in the hospital, but also a thrill to get to meet the little girl who had received Ryan's heart. Their Ryan had given part of himself to another child who would have lost her life. Now their Ryan's heart kept Polly Nash alive.

"We'd love to meet her, Mrs. Nash."

"Please, call me Becky. We can come by your house if you'd like. Royal isn't too far from where we'll be on the interstate. I know this is rather short notice, but we changed some plans and now we'll be driving where we can stop by next Tuesday if that is convenient. Would Tuesday afternoon be possible?"

"Yes, that would be perfect. We're at Knox Acres Ranch, just outside town. I can tell you how to get here."

They finished making the arrangements and ended the call. Emily remembered the young mother—a pretty blue-eyed blonde in her early twenties. Jason Nash, her tall brown-haired husband, was an accountant with a big company in Denver. One of the doctors had approached them about the transplant, and later, after they agreed, they met the parents. But Emily and Tom had never met Polly. Now that was going to change on Tuesday afternoon.

She started to call Tom to tell him, but she decided she'd rather tell him in person. And she was curious about the guesthouse. She hadn't been inside since he'd moved there after their separation.

She didn't know if he had changed it, spreading out and making a new home for himself. Or maybe he'd just left it the way it was.

She basked in the sunshine as she made the short walk across the yard and wide driveway. The guesthouse was a much smaller, far simpler house than the mansion, with a friendly warmth to it that she'd never felt the large house had. When she arrived, she crossed the porch to the open door. The screen door was closed, so she knocked on that.

"Come in," Tom called.

She stepped inside. "Where are you?" She looked around the living room that looked exactly like it always had after visitors had come and gone. The front room was immaculate and did not appear lived in.

"I'm in my office."

She had no idea where he had made an office, but she followed the sound of his voice and then saw him in the big master bedroom. He was on a ladder in the closet rummaging around on a shelf. Boxes and papers were strewn at his feet.

"I'm glad to see signs of someone living in here since you've been doing so for the past year. But you don't have much in the way of excess anything."

"I don't need much."

"Can you come down from there? I want to talk to you."

He paused and looked at her, and then came down a step and jumped the rest of the way.

He frowned as he faced her. "This must be something serious."

"It is. I need to talk to you."

He held out his hand. "Let's go in the living room and we can sit."

"I don't know that we need to sit to talk," she said, walking back into the front room and turning to face him. "I got a phone call. And I'm worried this might bring up some painful memories for us."

"Who called? This sounds important," he said.

"It is important. It was from Becky Nash."

Ten

Tom's hand stilled. "Why did she call us? Is the little girl all right?" he asked.

"Yes, she's fine. Her mother called because they are driving through Texas and asked if we would like to meet Polly. They are going to stop by here next Tuesday afternoon."

He looked away, his jaws clamped shut while he was silent. Finally he faced her again. "That is a big deal. We're going to meet the little girl who has our son's heart."

Silence stretched between them again, and Emily had a sinking feeling that a lot of their old problems were about to return, ending the fragile friendly truce.

"Would you rather I had told them not to come?"

He flinched and shook his head. "No. You did the right thing. We should meet her. I just keep thinking that part of Ryan is still a living organ, that there's part of him still here."

"And keeping another child alive. Tom, Ryan has given life to this little girl."

Tom wiped his eyes. "I know that. And that's what we wanted and it's good, but it doesn't make our loss lighter or lessen the hurt of losing Ryan one damn degree. It brings the loss all back in a way. We should meet her, but that doesn't make it easy." He turned his back to her and she knew he wiped his eyes again.

And she knew she couldn't comfort him and he didn't want her to try. He had turned his back on her and was shutting her out of his life.

She hurt more than ever and suspected the last little vestige of her marriage was shattering.

In spite of their time together, the quiet hours spent on Uncle Woody's porch just talking about each other's plans, Emily could tell that this reminder of their loss had thrown them back to the way it used to be. To when they had been estranged and avoided each other.

She knew he didn't want her there, so she walked quietly out of the guesthouse and crossed back to the main house, barely able to see for her tears.

It was definitely over between them. She could

tell when Tom turned his back on her that had been a final goodbye.

She had been wrapped in a false sense of happiness when he had lived in the old house with her and helped her get it back in shape. That was over and all the hurt over the bus wreck and loss of their son had returned. And it would always come back. There would be reminders through life and she and Tom needed to let go and try to rebuild their lives.

She loved Tom and she couldn't imagine ever loving anyone else, but her marriage to him was over. She suspected she would not see him again until the Nashes arrived on Tuesday.

She cried as she walked back to the mansion. But she felt she had known all along the day would come when they would go back to avoiding each other and Tom would sign the divorce papers.

She decided that she would pack and choose what she wanted to have moved to her house in Royal so she could go as soon as the Nashes left.

She entered the empty, silent house, wanting to be back in town and away from so many painful memories here.

She thought of the fun times she and Tom had had over the past days. The evenings they'd spent on the porch, just talking. They had found joy in each other again and she was beginning to have hope. Tom was the most wonderful man she had ever known and she had fallen in love with him all over again. And now she was hurting all over again.

She didn't feel like having dinner and Tom didn't show, so she put the casserole back in the refrigerator and went out to the sprawling patio to sit where she could look at the spring flowers in the yard and the big blue swimming pool with its sparkling fountain. It was a cool March evening and she would rather sit outside.

She would borrow one of the ranch trucks to take some furniture back with her. Tom wouldn't care what she took or what she left. She doubted whether he would ever live in the main house again, and she didn't want to.

She put her head in her hands to cry. She had lost them both—Ryan and Tom.

She cried quietly as she sat there in the dusky evening, looking at the fountain and feeling numb. She gazed beyond the pool. Silence enveloped her. Occasionally she could hear the wind, a soft sound, the only sound. As if the entire world was at peace. She knew better. It wasn't, and neither was her little corner of it. But the illusion was nice.

"Did you eat dinner?"

She heard Tom's deep voice from the doorway and turned around. He stood in the door with his hands on his hips.

"No. Do you want any?"

"No. I'll stay at the guesthouse tonight."

"I thought you probably would. I'll get my car tomorrow so I can take it back to Royal when I go."

When he didn't say anything else, she finally glanced over her shoulder to see if he stood watching her. She was alone. He had gone, and she wondered if they would ever again be relaxed and compatible the way they had been these past weeks.

Long after dark she went inside and began to gather scrapbooks and small things she wanted to take to Royal. There was nothing to hold her here at the ranch.

She propped up the pillows in her bed and sat against them on top of the covers to look through the old scrapbooks. But they made her sad, so she finally scooted down in bed to go to sleep.

Tom lay awake in the dark. As long as he and Emily were together, there would be reminders of their tragic past, some little moments and some big ones, like the Nashes' visit. Their visit would tear Emily up. It would probably tear him up just as much. He wanted them to come by, but it was going to hurt and be difficult to deal with. It also brought all the memories swarming back, the pain, the fear, the terrible wreck and panic that had consumed him. His inadequacy, his failure to protect the two he loved most—that's what always tore him up.

He couldn't ever forget carrying his son's little body, holding Ryan, which was like holding ice, against his heart, praying for him, unaware of his own injuries until much later. And then the decision to donate Ryan's organs to save another child—to save other parents from going through what they'd suffered.

Tom wiped his eyes. As long as he and Emily were together, they would always have moments when the memories and pain would return full force.

The loss was devastating and it didn't get easier. They had moved on, but the hurt of missing little Ryan…that never changed. Tom knew that if he lived to be one hundred, he would still shed tears over his baby.

The Nashes' upcoming visit complicated the healing process for him. In a way, it was a stark reminder that he had failed Emily when he failed to save Ryan. He had loved her with his whole heart and still loved her in so many ways, but he just didn't know how to make it up to her. Tom was certain Emily would be better off without him in her life.

If they both started with new friends, new homes, new everything—new loves in their lives, even— maybe each day wouldn't be filled with pain and loss and sorrow.

Tuesday would be tough. He dreaded the day,

but if he had taken the Nashes' call, he would have done the same thing Emily had and agreed to meet with them. Even though he knew it would be more heartache, he wanted to see the little girl who had Ryan's heart beating in her chest and giving her life.

Just the thought caused a knot in his throat. After Ryan, he had never been able to handle death and dying as well. Maybe it added to his heartache to have Jeremy's death so soon after losing Ryan.

Sleep wasn't going to come easily, probably not at all, but it wouldn't be his first sleepless night. Tom put his hands behind his head and looked out the open window at the stars. The divorce hung over them, and he wanted to go ahead and get it over and done with.

This living together in the same house again was gearing up to cause another big hurt for both of them. He ought to get out and let her go on with her life.

All the basic things were lined up to get done on Emily's old house. Nathan would send someone around to check on her, just like they were doing for Natalie. He and Emily needed to go ahead with their divorce.

Divorce was going to hurt because Emily was part of his life and it was like cutting into himself, but it would be best for both of them, definitely better for her.

Would seeing Polly Nash tear them both up? Ryan's heart still beat—that was the most amazing thing. Little Polly Nash could live because she had Ryan's heart. They would meet her Tuesday afternoon—and for just a little while part of Ryan would once again be with them, at the only home Ryan had known. Tom stared through the window. It would be another day he would remember as long as he lived. So would Emily.

On Tuesday morning, Tom showered and got dressed in a navy Western-style shirt, jeans and his best black boots. When he was finished, he combed his hair and left the guesthouse.

At noon, he walked over to the mansion and rang the bell. When Emily didn't come to the door, he stepped inside.

"Emily?" he called. He heard her heels as she approached in the hall. Then she entered the room and he couldn't get his breath as he looked at her. Her wavy honey-brown hair fell loosely around her face. She wore little makeup, but had a natural beauty he loved. She wore a sheer pale blue top over a pale blue silk cami and white slacks with high-heeled blue sandals.

"You take my breath away, you look so beautiful."

"Thank you," she said quietly. "I think that

should be my line, only substitute 'handsome' for 'beautiful.' You're the one who is dazzling."

"I'm not sure you have ever realized how beautiful I think you are."

"It's nice to hear you say that to me. I won't forget." She smiled, but there was a sad look in her eyes.

"I want to do this, and at the same time, I know it's going to hurt like hell."

"I know," she whispered. "You might as well come in and sit. You're a little early, and they may have trouble finding the ranch."

They walked into the formal living room and she sat in a dark blue wing chair while he went to the window to look out at the drive.

"This week I think we should go ahead with the divorce," Tom said quietly. "I think each of us will be better off. Reminders like today will always bring the pain back, and I just don't think we're equipped to deal with it together."

"I think we're dealing with it okay, Tom. Some things will fade as the years go by."

"We're better off just starting anew." He turned to face her. "You said you don't need me to stay with you in Royal, so I've talked to Nathan and he'll send someone around to check on you."

"Thank you."

"Will you be all right there alone?"

"Yes, I will," she said, smiling, sitting back in

the chair and crossing her long legs, which momentarily captured his attention and made him forget everything else.

"I told you I'd deal with the roofers, and I think I can get them out by the first of next week. How's that?"

"It will be fine. Thank you."

He gazed at her, thinking she was being very polite, which meant she was keeping a tight rein on her feelings. She was probably upset about meeting the Nashes' daughter. He turned back to the window. He needed to get through meeting Polly Nash. Get through the divorce. Maybe then he would find some peace in life.

He saw a car approaching and he doubled his hands into fists. Once again, he asked himself why he hadn't died in place of his son. Emily might not have wanted that, but he did. And why hadn't he died instead of Jeremy, who was within yards of him when he took the enemy fire? Jeremy had had so much to live for.

Frowning, Tom watched the car approach, wondering about those two situations that he had survived. He had better do something useful with his life to make up for the fact that Ryan's and Jeremy's had been cut short.

Emily followed Tom to the front porch and they stood waiting to greet the family as they stepped out of their gray van. A slender woman with straight hair got out as her husband walked around the car to her. He was in tan slacks and a tan knit shirt. He held the door as his daughter stepped out. Polly Nash was a pretty little girl with brown hair and hazel eyes with thick brown lashes—the same coloring as Ryan. She stood politely with her mother and held a wrapped package in her hands.

"Mr. and Mrs. Knox, we're so glad to see you again. This is our daughter, Polly," Becky Nash said by way of greeting.

"Please just call us Tom and Emily," Emily said.

"And you can call us Becky and Jason," Polly's mother replied.

"Come inside," Tom said and held the door.

When they were all in the formal living room, Emily invited them to take a seat. "Thanks for calling us. Are you vacationing?"

"Yes," Jason Nash said. "We're on our way back to Colorado now and thought we'd stop because we were passing so close by."

"Polly has something for you," Becky said and nudged her daughter, who smiled shyly and took the present to Emily.

"Thank you, Polly," Emily said, smiling at the little girl. "How old are you?"

"I'm eight. I'm in the third grade."

"That's great. Third grade is a good year. Tom, come open this with me."

The package was wrapped in light blue paper with a big silver-and-blue ribbon tied in a huge bow. Tom slipped it off the package and Emily carefully undid the pretty wrapping paper. "Did you wrap this, Polly?"

"No, ma'am. Mom did," she said, glancing at her mother, who was smiling.

When they unwrapped the package, there was another in brown mailing paper and tape addressed to a school. Emily handed it to Tom, who took out his pocketknife and carefully cut into the brown paper. When he was done, he pushed the paper away and held up a framed picture of a schoolroom with a picture of a plaque on the wall. The plaque had a picture of Ryan in one corner.

Looking more closely at the plaque, Emily read aloud. "'This Jefferson music room is built, furnished and maintained in loving memory of Ryan Knox of Royal, Texas.'"

"We've done that in your son's memory at Polly's school in Colorado."

"Thank you so much," Emily said. "That is touching and kind of you."

"We want to express our thanks to your son and to you folks in some way that's permanent. You gave our Polly back to us, gave her a chance at life."

"That's a fine memorial," Tom said. "Thank all three of you."

Emily gazed at Ryan's smiling picture. "This is a lovely memorial, and it means so much to Tom and me. Hopefully, we'll get to visit the school and see this," she said, smiling at the Nashes.

Tom turned to Polly. "Do you have a music class?"

"Yes, sir," she answered politely. "I'm learning to play the violin and I take piano lessons. I like my books and I like my piano lessons," she said, smiling.

"She has lots of friends at school, too," Becky added.

"Have you ever been on a ranch?" Tom asked.

Polly shook her head. "No, I haven't."

"Want to see the barn and the horses?"

She looked at her parents. "I think that's a yes," her dad said and stood. "I'll go with you and we'll look a little." He held out his hand and Polly took it. It reminded Emily of how she used to hold Ryan's hand, and she felt a tug on her heart.

Tom walked out with them, sounding friendly and cheerful, telling Polly about the ranch, but Emily wondered what his cheer was costing him.

"She's a sweet little girl," Becky said. "And I can't say enough how thankful we are—you've given our little girl life," she said, getting tears in her eyes. "That memorial is just a token gesture. We're looking into a college scholarship. Whatever we do, you'll be notified. We wanted to come here to show our gratitude in person."

"We're thrilled that Ryan's heart is giving her life," Emily said.

"I pray for you and your husband every day, and I give thanks that we are blessed to have our little girl. We just owe all of that to you and your husband."

"It's a miracle of science, and I'm thrilled we could help. Polly seems so sweet and bright."

Emily sat and talked to Becky until the others came back, Polly skipping ahead of the men. Emily's heart clutched again as she watched her.

After Polly told her mother about the three horses she had seen, Becky looked over Polly's head at Emily. "We have a lot of miles and should go, but before we do, would you like to feel her heartbeat? We've talked to her about it and she knows where she got her heart and she's happy for you to feel it beating."

Emily stood and crossed the room. "Is it all right if I touch you, Polly?"

Polly smiled and nodded. Emily put her hand on Polly's chest and felt the steady beat of the heart that had given life to her son. For an instant she experienced a renewed tie to her child. Tears filled her eyes.

Emily turned away, wiping at her tears. "Tom,"

she said. He stood close, and she took his hand and placed it on Polly's small chest.

"That's part of Ryan," he whispered and turned away. Becky wiped her eyes, too.

"We can never tell you what your gift has meant to us except that our Polly wouldn't be here with us today if it hadn't been for your Ryan. We're sorry for your loss. We are so grateful for your gift of life for Polly."

Emily looked into Polly's hazel eyes. "Thank you," she said softly. "Polly, thank you. You share a special tie with our little baby. Thank you." Emily moved away.

She and Tom went out with the Nashes to see them off. Standing on the drive waving as they drove off, Emily knew they would not see each other again.

Without waiting for Tom, she turned and went inside, walking to the kitchen to get a drink of water. She put her head in her hands and cried.

When she felt composed, she went back to the formal living room but found it empty. She walked out to the porch, but Tom was nowhere around. She looked at the guest cottage down the drive and saw no sign of him, but she suspected he was already there and she wouldn't see him again today. She had seen Tom's tears and knew he would be hurting badly.

Once again, she thought about her losses—of

her son and her husband, the only man she had ever loved or ever would love. But he was as lost to her as Ryan. Next would come the divorce, and then she didn't know if she would ever see him again.

She felt as if she was losing him for the second time, but this time, it would be permanent. She went to the bedroom where she was staying.

Soon Tom would be out of her life. She would have to make her own life.

She walked through the house to go upstairs and movement caught her eye. She realized Tom was outside in the back. He was standing on the patio, looking at the pool or the yard or something beyond him. She went out.

"I thought you had gone home."

"Not yet, but I'm going. I wanted to wait until the Nashes were gone." He wiped his eyes. Once again, there was a time she would have gone to him and put her arms around him. Now she knew he really wouldn't want her to do that. The wall was back between them.

He turned around to face her. His eyes were red, and she guessed hers probably were, too. "I think it's time for that divorce. We'll each be better off."

"I know, Tom. It's all right," she said. She looked at his broad shoulders and wondered if he was right. "I'll go back to Uncle Woody's tomorrow. If you can get someone to help me, I'd like to move a few things from here. Can I borrow a pickup?"

"Don't ask stuff like that. Do whatever you damn please. We share this ranch. I'll get two guys to help and you take anything and everything you want. You know how much this house means to me."

That hurt, because this house was where they had spent some wonderful years and it was the only home Ryan had known except Uncle Woody's.

"Thank you for all you did for me in Royal."

"I'll keep up with the window guys, also the floor people and the roofers. The floors should be done in two weeks. I'll check and let you know." He stood looking at her. "I'm going back to the guesthouse. What time do you want the guys here tomorrow?"

"I should be ready at about ten o'clock. I'll take some things. I may want to come back and get some more."

"Sure. Do what you want. Let me know if you need help." He looked at her a long time and turned away, passing her and going inside. She suspected he walked straight through and out the front and was headed to the guest cottage.

She went in, walking to the window to watch, and saw she was right. He walked with that straight back that people in the military develop. With each step he was walking out of her life.

She thought about Ryan's heart beating in Polly's chest. Her baby's heart—still beating, giving life to another child. Longing for Ryan, to hold him again and hear his laughter, swamped Emily. Longing for Tom quickly followed, to have his strong arms around her, his solid reassurance. She put her head in her hands and cried, aware she was losing Tom now even though she still loved him with all her heart. They'd had unhappy moments and she thought their love had crumbled, but she realized that was one more mistake. She loved him and she always would.

When she had calmed down, she locked up and went upstairs to sit on the balcony of the big master bedroom and cried some more. She hurt over both of them and she knew she would continue to hurt.

The next day she called Tom and didn't get an answer. She selected furniture she wanted and called their foreman, Gus. He already knew she was taking furniture to the house in Royal and he had three guys to help and two pickups and they were ready when she was.

Wondering where Tom was, she told Gus to send the men over. In a short time they were on the drive by the back door. She knew all three— Bix Smith, Ty Green and Marty Holcomb.

She showed them which pieces of furniture to

pack up. Tom didn't want anything to do with the house, so she took what she wanted.

She drove her car to Royal behind the two pickups and they spent the morning unloading furniture. The men left before noon, and when she was alone, she looked around, remembering Tom in every room and the happiness she'd had while they worked on the renovations together. The time had been good, but why couldn't life ahead be filled with a lot more good times? They had been through the worst. She stood gazing down the hall, seeing Tom there, smiling, flirting with her, making her laugh. Why were they getting a divorce when they had so much between them that was wonderful and fulfilling?

Thinking about their future, she drove down Main Street, turning on the block where her studio was located. As she stepped out of her car, the enticing smell of baking bread assailed her and she remembered Tom buying two loaves and eating half of one himself that night. She went into the bakery and bought two more loaves. She could always freeze them if she didn't eat them.

She went into her studio to pick up her mail and saw two other proofs of Tom's pictures on her desk. She picked one up and looked at him. "I love you," she whispered.

And that's when it hit her.

"We can't give up what we have," she said.

"We're not going to get a divorce, Tom Knox, because life with you is too awesome. It's way too marvelous to give up." She sat there staring at his picture. She didn't want a divorce. They'd had wonderful moments in the past weeks they were together. They had weathered the worst and survived and they still could enjoy each other's company.

She was going back to the ranch to find Tom and tell him she didn't want the divorce. She still had clothes at the ranch, so she didn't have to go home and get anything.

As she drove back to the ranch, she missed Tom and thought about the happiness they'd had together. Their love had moments when it was so great. She also thought about their lovemaking, which had been exciting and bound them together closer than ever. She wasn't ready to give up on their marriage. Not after the time she had spent with him.

But there was still the question of children. She thought about Tom as a father. He needed children in his life. She did, too. He was willing to adopt and he was right—they both would love any child in their lives. Why had she been so opposed to adoption? If she'd only agreed to adopt, this divorce wouldn't be looming in her life. Another big mistake she had made. But mistakes could be fixed sometimes. She hoped it wasn't too late.

As soon as she turned onto the ranch road, she

called Tom, but he didn't answer. She didn't see his pickup at the guesthouse when she passed it, so he must be out on the ranch.

She decided to stay at the mansion until she reached him. She tried the rest of the day and that night, but when she still didn't get him at midnight, she wondered if he had stopped taking her calls.

She slept little that night, pacing the floor and thinking about Tom, their past and their future.

By morning she was firmly set in her opinions about their future.

She didn't intend to walk away and lose him, because for the past few weeks, he had acted like a man in love. And she was definitely in love with him. She had fallen in love with him when she was sixteen and she had never stopped loving him.

She had made mistakes that might still cost her the marriage—like being so uptight about getting pregnant. Tom was right and they should just adopt. He was wonderful with any kids he was ever around.

Had he already signed the divorce papers?

It didn't matter. They could marry again. She wasn't giving up, because the days they had spent together had been a reunion for them, binding them together stronger than ever. He thought when they were together, they compounded the hurts. They might sometimes, but they definitely did not compound the bad times often.

Life had rough times, and Tom was tough enough to weather them. And so was she. Together they would do better at getting through them.

She showered, brushing out her long wavy hair and pulling on a red T-shirt, jeans and boots. She left to find him, walking to the guesthouse. He wasn't there, so she had called Gus, who said he hadn't seen Tom but thought he was still on the ranch.

She stood in front of the guesthouse and then she thought about where she might find him. She drove to the most beautiful spot on the ranch, a gradual slope that had a winding, shallow stream along the bottom. There were big oaks planted inside the small area that had a white picket fence around it. It was the plot of land she and Tom had picked out together for the cemetery where Ryan was buried, with a marble angel standing beside the marble headstone and a bank of blooming Texas Lilac Vitex on either side. Tom stood in the shade of one of the oaks with his pickup parked outside the fence.

When he saw her coming, he turned to face her and waited as she came through the gate.

He had on his black Stetson and a black cotton shirt, along with jeans and black boots. He looked wonderful to her.

"I was just about to leave to find you. I figured

I'd have to drive to Royal. I thought you went back to town."

"I did, but I came back. I thought I would find you here at the family cemetery. This place holds so much meaning for us."

"It's quiet out here and I can think about Ryan and about us, the past, the present—these days we've spent together. Think about this miracle of another little child having Ryan's heart that is givng her life."

"I know you used to come out here and just stay for a while."

"For me, it brings up so many good memories. Working on your house together, we added some more good moments."

As he stepped closer, he raised an eyebrow. "Why were you looking for me?"

A breeze tugged at her hair as she faced him.

"Will you come home with me?"

She saw the flare of surprise in his eyes. "I love you, and I don't want a divorce," she said. "Ever since I received the email from Maverick, you have acted like a man in love. We've had a lot of love between us, and I'm not ready to give up on this marriage." She hugged him tightly. "I know I've made mistakes, Tom, but we can work through the problems."

He wrapped his arms around her to kiss her, a kiss that was an answer by itself. Trembling, she clung to him and kissed him back while joy filled her because he would never kiss her this way if he was going to divorce her.

He released her slightly, letting his hands rest on her shoulders again. "Before we go any further, there's something I have to say." His expression was solemn and suddenly she wondered if she had guessed wrong, that his possessive and responsive kiss was goodbye.

Cold fear wrapped around her again. "What is it?"

"Ah, Em, I'm so sorry. I failed you both, you and Ryan. I couldn't save him. I failed you then in the worst way," Tom said, looking beyond her.

"You didn't fail me. You didn't fail him, either. Don't blame yourself when you are blameless."

"Yes, I did. I should have saved him."

"You couldn't. The doctors said he died from the trauma caused by his injuries in the bus," she said. "You didn't fail me or Ryan, because you did the very best you could. All of Ryan's life, you were an amazing father, and Ryan wanted to be just like you."

"I've always felt I failed you both. I don't know, Em—"

"Well, I know what I want and what I need. Our marriage has been good again—joyous, sexy, productive. We've been best friends and enjoyed each other's company, helped each other. We can do this. I'm not giving up on our marriage," she said, squeezing him tightly as if by holding him she could keep him from doing anything to end their union.

She looked up at him and he brushed her hair from her face to gaze into her eyes.

He stepped back and reached into his jeans pocket, struggling to pull something out. "That's why I was going to town. I wanted to find you and tell you that I don't want the damn divorce. I love you with all my heart and I need you in my life."

Tears of joy filled her eyes as she hugged him. "I love you. We can get through life together. Tom, I love you so."

Wrapping his arms around her, he kissed her again and this time her heart pounded with joy. He leaned away.

"You were always so strong," he said. "Too strong. I didn't think you needed me anymore."

"Yes, I do. I need you desperately. I'm unhappy without you. And I'm complete when we're together. Tom, there will be problems, but we can work through them. I love you. I need you." She looked into his hazel eyes that she loved, eyes that could melt her and at other times give her strength. "There will always be problems. That's life, but we're better at handling them when we're together. I love you and I need you."

"I love you more than you'll ever know and I

want to spend my life trying to show you." He released her and held out his hand. "I got this for you after we saw the Nash family."

Surprised, she examined the small velvet box. She couldn't imagine what he was giving her. She looked up at him and he smiled.

"Are you going to see what your present is?"

"Yes," she said, taking the box to open it. Inside was a tangle of a piece of jewelry. She picked it up and gasped as a necklace shook out in her hand. It was a golden heart pendant on a thin gold chain that was covered with diamonds.

"Oh, my heavens, Tom. It's beautiful."

"It's because of Ryan giving life with his heart to little Polly Nash. That holds meaning for both of us. It's a locket."

"Let me see. This is gorgeous—" She gasped when she opened the locket. "Tom, this is wonderful. I'll treasure this always," she said, hugging him again and kissing him longer this time while he held her tightly in his embrace.

She leaned away and held the locket up so they could both look inside at the picture of Ryan smiling into the camera. "You selected this locket for me. You must have changed your mind right after you told me we should go ahead with the divorce."

"It didn't take long. I've spent a year living in the guesthouse alone and then we've had this fantastic time together. No matter what we go through, I want you with me. I thought about it and I've loved you always. You're the only woman for me for the rest of my life. I love you. I'd give my life for you. I've loved you since you ran into my car when we were sixteen. And, Em, you worry so about having my child—"

"We can adopt. You're right. I watched you with the Valentine kids and I played with them and if we adopt, we'll love them like our own. We both would love any child we raised. Whatever you want to do. We can go without kids. There are loads of kids we can help without raising them—through reading programs, starting a ranch camp for kids, playing ball, you know, things you can help with and so can I."

He studied her. "You've got this all figured out, haven't you?"

"I'm desperate. I don't want to lose you, because I love you with all my heart. And you have never failed me, Tom. Never. You couldn't save Ryan. I couldn't save Ryan. The doctors couldn't save him. But you didn't fail me. You tried all you could."

"You're sure?" he asked.

"With all my heart. Please put my locket on me." She handed him the necklace and turned so he could fasten it at the back of her neck. "You really got this since we saw the Nashes?"

"I have a jeweler in Dallas. I sent a text, he sent

me pictures of what he had. I picked out this one and told him I wanted it delivered yesterday."

"Oh, my word. Someone from the jewelry store drove this to you?"

"That's right. I didn't want to wait. We've been separated way too long, my love."

She turned to face him. "This is wonderful, Tom, but most of all is knowing you'll be in my life."

"Baby, you're all that I need, and I'll spend the rest of my life making that clear to you. Em, I've thought all this time that you were angry because I failed you—"

"Never. We've both made big mistakes, but we've survived them and some of them we're able to let go and try to forget. They're not part of our lives any longer." She slipped her arms around him. "I'm so happy. I love you with all my heart. I know we'll be all right."

"I know we will. But how the hell do you undo a divorce?"

"I'm leaving that one to you. Oh, how I love you. I'll show you, too. It's time to leave here and go home. Oh, my heavens, we don't have a home," she said, frowning as she looked up at him. "You can't be a rancher and live in Uncle Woody's house in Royal. Neither of us wants to live in the mansion. We're not both living in the guesthouse."

Tom held her with his arms around her waist as

he smiled at her. "It's just another problem we'll work out. What do you think about finishing your Royal house? Then that will be our town house and you can still work in town part of the week if you want. And maybe it's time for a redo of ranch house. Or we can demolish it if you want and start over."

"We'll talk about that one—I vote for the redo because we have good memories there. I'll live on the ranch with you and maybe drive into town and keep the studio open by appointment only. But come home with me now," she said. "I've got two new loaves of bread for you in the car. How's that? And maybe some fun in the bedroom?"

"You've got a deal." Laughing, he pulled her into his embrace. "But I don't want to wait to show you how much I've missed you. We're not driving to Royal now. We're going to live in the guesthouse for a little while. I'll tell Gus we're going to Royal and he's in charge, but today, I don't want to drive any farther than our guesthouse. I have plans for us and that bread."

She laughed, looking into his eyes and seeing the happiness mirrored there that she felt.

"Tom, I'm not sure I felt this excited on our wedding day."

"It's a bigger deal now, Em. We know what we lost, what we almost lost and what we have. Our love is the essential part of our lives and we have our memories of Ryan to share. I want to spend every day of the rest of my life trying to show you how much I love you."

His words thrilled her as much as the look in his eyes. She stood on tiptoe and he leaned closer to kiss her while he embraced her.

Joy poured into her that there wouldn't be any divorce. She loved him—always had and always would. As she returned his kiss, she thought their future was filled with promise and hope.

* * * * *

August 2017: TEMPTED BY THE WRONG TWIN by USA TODAY *bestselling author Rachel Bailey.*

September 2017: TAKING HOME THE TYCOON by USA TODAY *bestselling author Catherine Mann.*

October 2017: BILLIONAIRE'S BABY BIND by USA TODAY *bestselling author Katherine Garbera.*

November 2017: THE TEXAN TAKES A WIFE by USA TODAY *bestselling author Charlene Sands.*

December 2017: BEST MAN UNDER THE MISTLETOE by USA TODAY *bestselling author Kathie DeNosky.*

* * *

If you're on Twitter, tell us what you think of Harlequin Desire! #harlequindesire

COMING NEXT MONTH FROM

Available April 4, 2017

#2509 THE TEN-DAY BABY TAKEOVER
Billionaires and Babies • by Karen Booth
When Sarah Daltry barges into billionaire Aiden Langford's office with his secret baby, he strikes a deal—help him out for ten days as the nanny and he'll help with her new business. Love isn't part of the deal...

#2510 EXPECTING THE BILLIONAIRE'S BABY
Texas Cattleman's Club: Blackmail • by Andrea Laurence
Thirteen years after their breakup, Deacon Chase and Cecelia Morgan meet again...and now he's her billionaire boss! But while Deacon unravels the secrets between them, Cecelia discovers she has a little surprise in store for him, as well...

#2511 PRIDE AND PREGNANCY
by Sarah M. Anderson
Secretly wealthy FBI agent Tom Yellow Bird always puts the job first. But whisking sexy Caroline away to his luxury cabin is above and beyond. And when they end up in bed—and expecting!—it could compromise the most important case of his career...

#2512 HIS EX'S WELL-KEPT SECRET
The Ballantyne Brothers • by Joss Wood
Their weekend in Milan led to a child, but after an accident, rich jeweler Jaeger Ballantyne can't remember any of it! Now Piper Mills is back in his life, asking for his help, and once again he can't resist her...

#2513 THE MAGNATE'S MAIL-ORDER BRIDE
The McNeill Magnates • by Joanne Rock
When a Manhattan billionaire sets his sights on ballerina Sofia Koslov for a marriage of convenience to cover up an expensive family scandal, will she gain the freedom she's always craved, or will it cost her everything?

#2514 A BEAUTY FOR THE BILLIONAIRE
Accidental Heirs • by Elizabeth Bevarly
Hogan has inherited a fortune! He's gone from mechanic to billionaire overnight and can afford to win back the socialite who once broke his heart. So he hires his ex's favorite chef, Chloe, to lure her in, but soon he's falling for the wrong woman...

She had to calm down.

She was going to see Jaeger again. Her onetime lover, the father of her child, the man she'd spent the past eighteen months fantasizing about. In Milan she hadn't been able to look at him without wanting to kiss him, without wanting to get naked with him as soon as humanly possible.

Jaeger, the same man who'd blocked her from his life.

She had to pull herself together! She was not a gauche girl about to meet her first crush. She had sapphires to sell, her house to save, a child to raise.

Piper turned when male voices drifted toward her, and she immediately recognized Jaeger's deep timbre. Her skin prickled and burned and her heart flew out of her chest.

"Miss Mills?"

His hair was slightly shorter, she noticed, his stubble a little heavier. His eyes were still the same arresting blue, but his shoulders seemed broader, his arms under the sleeves of the black oxford shirt more defined. A soft leather belt was threaded through the loops of black chinos.

The corner of his mouth tipped up, the same way it had the first time they'd met, and like before, the butterflies in her stomach crashed into one another. She couldn't, wouldn't throw herself into his arms and tell him that her mouth had missed his, that her body still craved his.

He held out his hand. "I'm Jaeger Ballantyne."

Yes, I know. We did several things to each other that, when I remember Milan, still make me blush.

What had she said in Italy? *When we meet again, we'll pretend we never saw each other naked.*

Was he really going to take her statement literally?

Jaeger shoved his hand into the pocket of his pants and rocked on his heels, his expression wary. "Okay, skipping the pleasantries. I understand you have some sapphires you'd like me to see?"

His words instantly reminded her of her mission. She'd spent one night with the Playboy of Park Avenue and he'd unknowingly given her the best gift of her life, but that wasn't why she was here. She needed him to buy the gems so she could keep her house.

Piper nodded. "Right. Yes, I have sapphires."

"I only deal in exceptional stones, Ms. Mills."

Piper reached into the side pocket of her tote bag and hauled out a knuckle-size cut sapphire. "This exceptional enough for you, Ballantyne?"

Don't miss
HIS EX'S WELL KEPT SECRET by Joss Wood,
available April 2017 wherever
Harlequin® Desire books and ebooks are sold.

And follow the rest of the Ballantynes with
REUNITED...AND PREGNANT, available June 2017,
Linc's story, available August 2017,
and Sage's story, available January 2018.

www.Harlequin.com

Whatever You're Into... Passionate Reads

Looking for more passionate reads from Harlequin®?
Fear not! Harlequin® Presents, Harlequin® Desire and
Harlequin® Blaze offer you irresistible romance stories
featuring powerful heroes.

◆HARLEQUIN *Presents*®

Do you want alpha males, decadent glamour and jet-set
lifestyles? Step into the sensational, sophisticated world of
Harlequin® Presents, where sinfully tempting heroes ignite a
fierce and wickedly irresistible passion!

◆HARLEQUIN® *Desire*

Harlequin® Desire novels are powerful, passionate and
provocative contemporary romances set against a backdrop of
wealth, privilege and sweeping family saga. Alpha heroes with
a soft side meet strong-willed but vulnerable heroines amid a
dramatic world of divided loyalties, high-stakes conflict and
intense emotion.

◆HARLEQUIN® *Blaze*

Harlequin® Blaze stories sizzle with strong heroines and
irresistible heroes playing the game of modern love and lust.
They're fun, sexy and always steamy.

Be sure to check out our full selection of books
within each series every month!

www.Harlequin.com

Turn your love of reading into rewards you'll love with
Harlequin My Rewards

HARLEQUIN®
A *Romance* FOR EVERY MOOD™

Love the Harlequin book you just read?

Your opinion matters.

Review this book on your favorite book site, review site, blog or your own social media properties and share your opinion with other readers!

Be sure to connect with us at:
Harlequin.com/Newsletters
Facebook.com/HarlequinBooks
Twitter.com/HarlequinBooks

Get 2 Free Books,
<u>Plus</u> 2 Free Gifts—
just for trying the Reader Service!